A Place to Belong

A Bindarra Creek Christmas Romance

Annie Seaton

This book is a work of fiction. Names, characters, places, magazine and incidents are the product of the author's imagination or are used fictitiously. Any resemblance to actual events, locales, or persons, living or dead, is coincidental.

Copyright © 2023 Annie Seaton

ISBN 9781923048164

ANNIE SEATON

Dedication

To Ian, my partner in life and love… with me in the place we belong.

A PLACE TO BELONG

Chapter 1

A country road . . .

Saturday, December 2nd 3.00 p.m.

Violet Valentine eased back on the accelerator of her brand-new four-wheel-drive ute as the gravel road descended into a small, shaded valley. A message had dinged on her phone as the vehicle whizzed effortlessly up the hill, but she hadn't had a chance to look at it as she concentrated on the unfamiliar—and rough—road. The phone had then rung twice before the phone service dropped out. She'd expected the mobile reception to be patchy out here in the northwest of New South Wales. She wasn't worried; she knew it would be her sister, Wendy, checking up on her, which she had done at this time every day for the past five days since Violet had left her home state and headed south across the border.

And with much criticism from her big sister.

"Why on earth would you leave a brilliant job with the best horse stud in the whole of

Queensland?" her sister had said. "You had a great salary, a job you loved, and fabulous rent-free accommodation. Honestly, Vi, I cannot understand your thinking sometimes."

Violet had shaken her head and lied to her sister for the first time in her life. "I'm twenty-eight years old, and I've worked since I left uni. I have a brand-new ute that will take me off-road and a sense of adventure. I'm going to see some of the country."

She didn't mention that she had a job interview in the Hunter Valley next week. It was unlikely, but if Brian, her ex-boss and former partner, did get in touch with Wendy, she wanted none of her plans shared, accidentally or otherwise. Wendy had no idea what Brian was like.

No one did; he was clever. He'd always treated her well when there was an audience.

"The last thing I want is to have no idea where you are," Wendy said. "I'll worry myself sick. I'll call every day."

"There's no need. I'm a big girl now, Wen. And I won't do anything risky."

"And what about Christmas? We'll miss you. Maybe you could fly home?"

"No, it's time I stood on my own two feet. I have no idea where I'll be in a month."

The teary farewell had been emotional for Violet as she had no intention of ever going back to Queensland.

"I'll fly down and visit you wherever you end up," Wendy had said with a frown when she'd asked how long Violet would stay away.

"Come and visit for my birthday, and maybe I'll come home for Christmas next year," Violet said. "If we plan that, we'll see each other at least once every year."

"I'll do it in comfort if I do visit you," Wendy replied. Rolling her eyes, she gestured to Violet's ute. "There is no way I could travel like that. That's what Jerry always wants to do A swag and a tent in the back of a ute."

"I know you, well." Violet pulled her sister in for a last hug and blinked to clear the tears that stung at the back of her eyes. "You love your business class flights and your five-star hotels. I love being in the bush. Besides, I have a very comfortable swag, a waterproof tent and a new four-wheel drive, everything I need. Did I show you the fabulous camp chair that I bought?"

"I'm not interested in a camp chair. Stop changing the subject. You just know that I'm going to worry about you."

Violet glanced back in the rearview mirror before she turned the corner at the end of Wendy's street and saw her sister wiping away tears.

Violet had shed many tears too over the past couple of weeks, but not all of them had been caused by the thought of leaving Brisbane and her family.

Last night she'd made good use of her new gear, camping east of Armidale at a national park campground. The weather had been kind, and being the only camper, she'd found the quiet and tranquillity she'd craved.

The morning mist had hovered over the valley below as she sipped her coffee and enjoyed the solitude. The song of bellbirds tinkled around her, and an echidna ambled across the grassy flat.

For the first time since she had found the courage to leave, calm trickled through Violet and she managed to put her worries aside. She would never have to see Brian Bailey again. More than anything—and Violet knew she had to get over what had happened—she had to rebuild her confidence. Brian had destroyed her self-esteem, not to mention her confidence in her ability to do her job well.

Last night when there had been phone service, she'd Googled the national parks between Armidale and the Hunter Valley.

The sound of the Akuna National Park to the west had appealed. The website informed her that visitors to the park based their 'exploration of the park around water activities, such as swimming, fishing, and kayaking. A wonderful spot for long, relaxed bushwalks, birdwatching, nature photography, and self-reliant camping and hiking'; the description sounded perfect for her needs, and she could make use of her small kayak that was on the back of the ute.

Once she'd packed up her campsite in New England this morning, Violet followed the dirt roads to the southwest. It was less than a hundred kilometres to the Akuna National Park and she'd stopped several times to look at the amazing views from the lookouts and to take some photos to text to Wendy.

So far, she hadn't seen any signs directing

her to the national park, and the navigation on her car couldn't seem to access the satellite, but she knew she was heading in the right direction.

The landscape around her gradually opened out as the trees thinned. For the last twenty kilometres or so, Violet had followed a ridgeline and caught occasional glimpses of a river winding below. According to the National Park website, the Akuna River bisected the national park, so she had to be close to the boundary of the park.

Taking a deep breath of appreciation, she gazed out onto the landscape; it was almost like a rural painting. To the east, emerald-green rolling hills filled her vision, obviously pasture for some of the sheep and cattle properties she knew were around the district. It seemed they had received a fair bit of rain out here over the winter as the pasture was green and lush. On one hill close to the road, she spotted some black horses in a well-fenced paddock.

The phone beeped again bringing her back to the present. She rolled her eyes and spotted a clearing on the other side of the creek at the bottom of the hill where she could pull over and check her messages. Wendy was being more persistent this afternoon. Violet knew it wouldn't be anyone else because she had changed her phone number.

As she went down the slight descent, the car shuddered and the gear changed with a loud clunk from beneath the car. She frowned; it was the first time it had done that. She'd run the car around the city and the hinterland for 1500 kilometres before packing up for her trip, so the motor had been run in before she'd set off. Brian had gone to a conference in Sydney for the week, so as soon as Violet got home from work each afternoon, she went for a long drive. Two days before he was due back, her car was parked in a secure parking station, packed and ready to go. Her plans were made and she texted him the day he was due home.

Don't call in tonight. I'm going to Wendy's. I'll see you at work tomorrow.

By the time she was due at work that day, she was over the border, with a new phone and phone number.

The descent levelled out, but the gearbox clunked again. This time, it made a grinding noise too. Horrendous noises continued to come from underneath the ute as she headed for the creek crossing.

Slowly entering the shallow water—it was crystal clear and easy to see the depth to the concrete causeway, Violet tried to ignore the grinding noise.

As she reached the middle of the wide creek, the car made one final loud clunk and then as she hit the brakes, the motor cut out. The water had got a little bit deeper and now came halfway up the tyres, and steam filled the air as the water lapped at the bottom of the engine.

"Great, just great," she muttered. The water wasn't flowing hard enough to push her vehicle over the causeway, so that wasn't a worry. Her immediate concern was what was wrong with her car. She sat there for a minute and tried her usual trick. Her uni friends had laughed when it was her fix for a computer problem: shut it down, wait for five minutes, restart. Violet always said she had the magic touch because, no matter what had happened, the computer always used to work when she did that.

She tried that technique with the vehicle, rolling down her window, turning the ignition off, waiting for five minutes, and then restarting. The steam settled, but every time the water slapped on the bottom of the motor, she could hear a sizzle.

As Violet waited, she reached for her phone and picked it up. She suspected there was no service at all, but she knew that the message that came in a while ago would still be there. She clicked on the message, and sure enough, it was from Wendy.

Don't forget to report in today.

She put the phone aside, put her foot on the brake and pressed the ignition. The engine turned over sluggishly but it didn't fire.

"Well, I do have a problem," she muttered.

No phone service, no access to the RACQ or whatever it was called here, and stuck in the middle of a creek. No way could she push the car herself.

She reached down and slipped her joggers and socks off; luckily, she was wearing shorts, so her clothes wouldn't get wet when she got out.

Making sure the handbrake was on, she tried to put the car in park, but the lever refused to budge. She pulled the slide to release the bonnet; if something had come adrift under there it might be easy to spot and fix.

If I'm lucky.

However, Violet had her doubts about these new, computer-assisted engines. They were very hard to diagnose, unlike in the old days with her first car when she could tighten a cable here, top up the oil there, and keep her old Holden ute running.

Nevertheless, after walking around to the front of the vehicle in knee-deep water and pushing the bonnet up. she still peered over the array of shiny shapes and pristine cables. It all looked fine; even if something was out of place, she didn't know this vehicle at all and wouldn't be able to identify what was wrong. She'd been in such a rush to get away before Brian came back from his conference, this was the first time she'd even looked under the bonnet

With a sigh, Violet closed the bonnet, walked carefully around to the driver's door and reached in for her joggers and socks. She hadn't passed any houses for the past half-hour or so, so she knew there was nothing behind her, apart from that horse farm about ten ks back. By the look of the landscape, she was probably in the Akuna National Park.

She walked across the creek deep in

thought; she'd check out the clearing and then retrieve her tent and swag from the back of the ute, and set up camp for the night.

She had plenty of fuel after filling up this side of Armidale, so it wasn't a fuel issue. The ominous sound from the gearbox was obviously the cause of the problem, and the computer system had shut the engine down before anything was damaged.

Unless it already was.

At least whatever the problem was would be fixed under warranty.

The immediate problem confronting her was getting the damn vehicle somewhere where it could be repaired.

Chapter 2

Joe Rossiter's farm.

Saturday, December 9th 3.00 p.m.

"Hello? Are you there, Joe?"

Joe Rossiter jumped and almost dropped the paint roller in his right hand. He leaned back and looked down the hall from the kitchen to the front door.

"Come on in, Holly."

He climbed down the ladder, and by the time he'd put the roller in the paint tray, Holly had walked down the hall carrying the gift basket he'd ordered for Jac and Ryan.

Joe had finished painting the living room before lunch, put all the furniture back, and then put the Christmas tree up and decorated it. He grinned; if you could call his effort of throwing tinsel on the she-oak in the bucket of sand, and putting a plastic gold star on the highest branch he could reach, decorating.

This weekend, his focus was on the house. He had months of work ahead and had to stop going about it as a hit-and-miss project. He needed a plan. Working as a builder's labourer, some knowledge should have rubbed off, but at first, Joe was too busy thinking about the land he'd bought to look very closely at the house.

But he'd made a plan and followed it through, and now the old farmhouse was looking great. He'd achieved a lot in the three months since he'd moved in painting through, new carpet, and polishing the floorboards in the three bedrooms and the living room. The kitchen had been a lot of work, especially working by himself. He'd spent last weekend installing new cupboards he bought at Bunnings in Tamworth, and this morning he'd finished painting the living room and then moved to the last room—the kitchen.

He smiled at Holly when she met him in the middle of the hall. "You're a lifesaver, Holly. Great idea and even a home delivery service."

Every year since Jaclyn had married his brother, Joe had had the same problem. He had no idea what to buy for them for Christmas. There was only so much hand cream and boxed hankies that a couple could use. It was easy enough to buy toys for Georgia; the post office always made sure there was something suitable there. Jaclyn seemed to have the knack of gifting him something useful every Christmas and birthday.

Holly's gift baskets were the answer to his problem. Last week in town, he'd spotted an ad on the community noticeboard for the gift baskets. He pulled out his phone and called the number on the flyer straightaway and was surprised when Holly David answered.

"Holly, it's Joe Rossiter. What are you doing selling gift baskets? I thought you were working at the hospital in Lismore."

"Is it that long since we last caught up at the pub? It's almost a year since I left there."

"Probably, I haven't been to the pub much lately." Joe had only been to the pub a couple of times since he'd bought the farm. No time and he was trying to save money. "Are you working in town now?"

"I've started my own business with the baskets, and while it gets going, I'm renting out a room in my place to help pay the bills."

"Good on you," Joe said. "I hope it goes well for you. I'll order your biggest size for Jaclyn and Ryan, please."

"A picnic basket or a gift basket?" Holly had asked.

Joe frowned. "You know Jac. You choose."

"Well, seeing as they're going away, I'd say the gift basket. Jac was really looking forward to their trip when I saw her at the Cyprus Café the other day. I couldn't get over how much Georgia's grown."

"She has grown. And yes, Jac is excited. They're leaving this week and that's why I want to give them their present this weekend."

Joe had organised to collect the basket in town on Saturday morning, but Holly had called last night to say she could drop it off

"I'm sorry to inconvenience you, Joe. I was wondering if I could drop the basket off at your new place tomorrow afternoon. You're out on the Armidale Road, aren't you? I'm sorry I won't—" Holly had started apologising, but Joe interrupted.

"No problem at all, Holly. Suits me down to the ground. I can stay home and paint all day now. I'll get a couple of rooms done, but are you sure it's not too far out of your way?"

Holly reassured him. "No, I have to come out your way anyway, so it's only a little detour to come down your road. How far along are you?"

"Exactly fifteen ks to the turnoff to the national park."

"I can find that. I'll see you about three, Joe."

Now Joe glanced up at the clock as she followed him into the living room. Holly was right on time. Her eyes crinkled in a happy smile as she spotted his Christmas tree with brightly wrapped parcels beneath it. She was a pretty girl, a blue-eyed brunette who was always smiling. They had some mutual friends and had spent some time out with the group at the pub over the last couple of years since he'd started visiting Ryan in Bindarra Creek before he too had moved here. When Holly wasn't working up at Lismore at the hospital, she came to the pub with some local friends.

When Joe had been working as a contract shearer, he'd spent most Saturday afternoons at the Riverside Pub, and when he'd moved to town to work with his brother, and Grant Cummings, the landscaper, he'd had joined the social cricket club at the hotel and that meant late fun nights in the bar after the Saturday games.

He hadn't signed up this year, because he'd known that he would be putting Saturdays into getting the property and the house sorted.

Joe frowned. Why was it that all his mates were finding partners and settling down, but he had never met anyone who had given him that spark? He had many female friends, both in Bindarra Creek and Tamworth. He'd had a few short relationships, but none of them had really met that expectation of the sort of woman he would like to settle down with one day.

When Ryan and Jaclyn got married and started a family, he'd been envious. He'd never seen his brother so happy.

Holly was a nice girl, and she was a good friend, but there was no spark. The same with Leah when she came to town last Christmas; he had been interested, they'd hit it off straight away and he'd taken her out to Ryan and Jac's for a barbeque, but again, no spark.

He frowned as he stared over the top of Holly's head at the Christmas tree. Maybe his standards were unrealistic.

But Joe knew that he would wait for real

love; he knew what he wanted. Ryan and Jac had a great relationship, and if he had to wait until he was forty to meet Mrs. Right, so be it.

Holly scratched her nose and looked at him. "What on earth are you thinking about, Joe? You look like you're off with the pixies."

He laughed and shook his head. "Must be the paint fumes. I've been locked up in the house all morning with a tin of paint. I'll put the basket under the tree."

"Nice tree. I love that you've got one when you live out here by yourself."

"It's a bit naff though, isn't it?" Joe pulled a face. "First time I've decorated a tree since Ryan and I were kids."

"It's great. I love the she-oak in a bucket of sand. To me, that's much more an Aussie Christmas than the green plastic or silver tinsel trees. Not that there's anything wrong with them. Each to his own, it's the spirit of Christmas that counts, isn't it? May I?" Holly pointed to the gold star that was leaning a bit drunkenly almost at the top of his tree.

"Go for it."

Joe folded his arms as she grinned at him and climbed onto the sofa, securing the star to a stronger and higher branch so that it actually graced the top of the tree rather than a sideways branch. Then she rearranged the strands of tinsel he'd pretty much thrown at the branches.

She stood back and smiled. "There you go. Much more balanced."

'Thank you. Much better.'

He looked at the gift basket that Holly had placed beside Georgia's presents. A wicker basket filled with much more than he'd expected. "That's huge. Have I paid you enough?"

"That's the one you ordered. It looks extra big because some of the jars are large.' Holly smiled. "There's clear cellophane scrunched up between the bottles, so it pads it out." She smiled. "I might have thrown in a couple of extra little things into your basket. Jac and Ryan are great people, and Ryan has done a lot of work for me and my family." Holly pointed to the bottles in the middle of the basket. "There's one hundred percent local produce in there. Fig and strawberry jam from Damien Forster's berry farm, wine from Storey Family Wines, local honeycomb, and gingerbread cookies. Don't you just love the smell of gingerbread cooking?" Her smile was contagious.

Joe chuckled. "I've never smelled gingerbread cookies baking."

"When I start baking them, it really starts to feel like Christmas." Holly's blue eyes sparkled with delight when she smiled, and Joe couldn't help being dragged into the Christmas spirit.

"I baked those myself," she said, "but there's also some Christmas tarts from the bakery."

Joe shook his head. "Will it keep? Ryan and Jac leave for the islands in a few days. They won't have time to eat it all before they go."

"It will." Holly bent down and picked up a couple of stray she-oak spikes off the floor. "I'd better get going, Joe. One more delivery and I'm done for the day. I'm sure I'll see you in town before Christmas at the pub or the Carols by Candlelight."

'You will. Thanks for coming out, Holly, and good luck with the new business." Joe walked her to the back door. "And thanks for fixing my tree."

Two hours later, he paused and listened for a moment before he ran the roller over the last corner of the kitchen. It sounded like rain on his tin roof. The last few days had been lovely, with clear days warming up quickly. His new veggie garden would appreciate a drop of rain.

Ryan and Jac had come out three weekends ago, and his sister-in-law had stood at the edge of the huge vegetable garden with her hands on her hips. "My goodness, Joe, are you going into market gardening? What are you going to do with all those vegetables?"

Joe replied, "I don't know, Jac. I just enjoy growing them."

"Well, you certainly have a green thumb."

The recent weather was helping his green thumb along very well. The only problem Joe was having was the deer that he had to keep out of his patch—they'd eaten the first batch of seedlings as soon as they'd sprouted a few weeks ago. Since then, he'd built a solid fence with the star pickets he found in the shed. Phil at the hardware store had spent a good half hour helping him choose the best fencing wire. He was a good salesman; Joe had come out of the store with a lot more than he'd intended to buy. Since the hardware store had expanded and moved out on the Tamworth Road you could just about get anything you needed there. Joe had been disappointed when he'd had to buy the flatpack kitchen in Tamworth; he liked to support local business as much as he could.

He climbed down off the ladder and took the paint tray and roller out to the original laundry where the old stone sink had come in handy for renovations. He washed them and put them on the back porch to dry overnight. On his way back inside, he stood at the back door and looked at the clouds rolling over from the west. There was blue sky behind them, and the rain had almost stopped; it was only a few spits now. He grabbed his boots and headed outside, whistling for his dog.

"Come on, Molly, are you up for a walk? I'm going for a ride."

Sam, the horse he'd inherited from the previous owners, waited in the paddock close to the house. Joe went back inside and grabbed a carrot to put in his pocket. Local gossip told him the old horse had been on the property his whole life, and that he stayed here had been a condition of each time the farm had sold. Whenever the property was sold, Sam went with the land, or the sale wasn't on. Joe knew that subsequent vendors and purchasers didn't have to stick to the arrangement of the original owners, but he'd been more than happy to take the big white horse.

Sam was a gentle old soul, and Joe rubbed his forelock as he threw a blanket over his back and put the bridle on him. He didn't mind being led and he knew better than to bother Molly. The one time she'd nipped at his hooves, she'd got a small kick in return, so she was wary of the old horse, even though Sam didn't have a nasty bone in his body.

Joe climbed onto his back and leaned over to open the gate.

"Come on, Sam, take me for a wander. We can check that boundary fence past the house." Sam had his regular route, and Joe had seen more of his property from the old horse's back than he had in his ute.

This afternoon, Sam headed north, and Joe wondered what was out that way. The back of his property shared a border with the Akuna National Park, and he hadn't been out that way yet; he had only driven out on the forestry road. It was too far to take old Sam for an exploration on horseback. One weekend, he'd saddle up

Misty, the new horse he'd bought from the Kendalls before they'd moved to the coast, and he'd head out for the day. When the house was done.

Ryan reckoned there was an old woolshed out that way from the 1920s. Apparently, he'd heard that all the Melbourne Cup winners from that time had been written up on the woolshed wall by the shearers of the time.

As they headed further into the bush, Joe whistled to Molly from time to time. The answering rustling of leaves let him know where she was. She wasn't far off having her pups, so he had to be careful of where she went.

He'd bought the property from a young couple who had purchased it for a lifestyle change. It had only taken them six months to realise the lifestyle was harder than they'd imagined. One hundred acres, a house that needed a total renovation, a stable, some small sheds, and cattle yards that were pretty much unusable. They needed demolishing and redoing if Joe had intended to put any cattle there, but he didn't. He planned to raise a small herd of sheep and look into the local wool industry.

His day jobs gave him more hours than Joe

wanted because he knew he needed to spend more time getting the property in order.

Contentment filled him as Sam followed Molly along the creek.

Chapter 3

Violet

Violet had her campsite almost set up with just one tent peg to hammer in. She sat back on her heels as perspiration ran down her back; it was humid and there was still no sign of a breeze. As the shadows lengthened, she looked up at the sky. The sun had slipped below the hills to the west, and the sky was transforming from a light mauve to a deep purple; the silver edging the clouds was quickly turning to gold setting up a spectacular show for her.

She'd checked the status of local fire bans earlier in the day, and due to the recent rain in the hills, the fire danger was moderate, but there was no fire ban yet. The only problem was that she wasn't sure if she was in the National Park or not, and if she was, she shouldn't be camping unless it was a designated campsite with fireplaces.

But the remains of a fire nearby reassured her that someone had camped here fairly recently; she would be very careful.

Once the last tent peg was secure, she ventured into the bush without any concern about encountering anyone.

She'd be grateful to see someone. Keeping an eye out for snakes, she walked a couple of hundred metres into the bush. She spotted a pile of firewood along the fence line, which seemed to belong to the property, so she concluded she might not be in the national park.

She collected enough firewood for a fire tonight and in the morning, keeping a watchful eye out for snakes and spiders as she lifted each dead branch.

With her campfire going, Violet was about to retrieve her small pan and open the camp fridge in the back of the ute when a beautiful golden Labrador emerged from the bush.

"Hello," she said. "Who are you, and where did you come from?" Having a domestic dog appear at her campsite reassured her that there must be a farmhouse nearby, which would make it easier to find a telephone to call for help in the morning.

The dog came closer, and Violet soon realised the dog was heavily pregnant. "Well, look at you," she said. "About to have a litter of pups. Where's your owner? You shouldn't be wandering out like this. Is your home just down the road a bit? It's not safe with cars on the road, girl."

She couldn't resist feeling the pup's belly. The metal tag on her collar told her the bitch's name was Molly, and she could feel at least half a dozen puppies in there. A whistle caught her attention as she stood.

"Molly, where are you?" A voice called from along the road, followed by another shrill whistle.

"I guess you're Molly," she said as the dog settled next to the fire. Violet checked the fire wasn't burning too high, and walked across the clearing onto the road.

A solid man who she assumed was the dog's owner sat astride a white horse that was ambling towards the clearing.

Violet waited as the horse and rider approached, feeling a little guilty about camping on what was probably private property without permission.

"Hello there," he called out. "Lovely night."

"Hi," Violet responded. "I hope I'm not

camping somewhere I shouldn't be."

"No, it's fine," the man reassured her. "I've noticed a few people camping in that little clearing over the last few weeks. It's fine as long as you don't leave your rubbish or set my bush on fire."

"I actually didn't plan to camp here," Violet explained. "I was heading for the national park. But I wasn't sure where the turn-off was. My navigation stopped working plus I had no phone service as a backup."

"Akuna is twenty-two ks from here. If it was lighter, you'd be able to see the hills above the river from here. The turnoff is fifteen ks past my farm," the man said as he jumped off the huge horse.

He walked over and extended his hand. "I'm Joe Rossiter."

"Violet Valentine," she replied, taking his hand and shaking it. His grip was firm and his skin was warm.

"Cute name, but I guess lots of people say that. I don't think I've ever met a Violet before."

She rolled her eyes. "It was my mum's favourite flower."

"Bit prettier than Joe. And I'm Joe, not Joseph, so I can't even claim biblical connections. Are you going to head to the national park tomorrow?"

Violet pulled a face, gesturing behind him. He obviously hadn't seen her ute parked in the middle of the creek.

At the same time, he looked around and said, "Where's your car? You're not one of those long-distance pushbike riders, are you?"

"Look behind you," she said, pointing again. He turned and frowned when he spotted her white ute parked in the middle of his creek.

"What's it doing in the creek??"

"It stopped and I couldn't start it. That's why I'm camped here."

"Fuel?" he asked.

"No. I filled it up less than a hundred ks back. It's a brand-new car and has only got 2000 ks on it. It made a couple of loud clunks and decided to stop. Then it wouldn't go into gear. I planned to walk for help in the morning if I couldn't get it started. Not that I imagine it will; I've tried to start it a couple of times tonight with no luck. I did see a farm not far back, but I thought it was too far to walk at this time of night, and I wasn't even sure if anyone lived there anyway."

A wide smile spread over Joe's face. "Well, you're in luck. My place is only a couple of ks down the road."

"Oh, that's a relief. I'll wander down tomorrow morning and use your phone if that's okay." Violet patted her pocket. "I've got no phone service here."

"I don't have a lot of it at my place either," Joe said. "It comes and goes on a whim. I don't know what it is—could be the wind, could be the sunshine, could be the clouds, but it's not very reliable."

"The joys of living in the bush," Violet said.

"Yep." Joe nodded. "Listen, instead of leaving your car in the creek overnight, I can ride back and get the tractor and pull it out."

"Oh, that would be great if it's not imposing too much."

"Not at all. It won't take me long to go back and drive it back here." He looked up at the darkening sky. "I wouldn't be happy about leaving it there because even though we've only had a bit of a shower, there's enough colour in those clouds to give us a downpour. And if we get enough, that creek will flow."

"Lucky you came along, Joe. Thank you," she said.

"I'll be back in half an hour at most."

As Violet sat by the campfire, she felt relieved that she wouldn't have to worry about seeking help the next morning. She had been lucky, and she smiled as she thought what an easy-going guy he was. Joe hadn't been at all judgemental, and it seemed like nothing was a problem.

Chapter 4
Joe

Joe hurried home, urging Sam to a faster pace than usual. The closer he got back to the farmhouse, the brilliant sky of this afternoon's sunset faded and the darker the sky got as towering clouds scurried in from the west. By the time he'd put Molly in her dog pen, checked her kibble was topped up, and put Sam in the stable, given him a quick wipe down, and thrown in some fresh hay, it was dark, and he could hear the rain splattering on the roof.

He hurried up the steps and into the house to get the tractor key; if this rain turned into anything, the creek would rise very quickly. He grabbed his oilskin in case the rain hit harder. The clearing Violet was camped on had gone under a couple of times in the early autumn when he'd first arrived, due to heavy spring rains.

As he started the tractor and headed off down to the creek, he thought back to what Violet said about the car not going into any gear. If the gearbox was cactus and they couldn't get it into neutral, the wheels wouldn't turn, and they'd have to drag the ute up the short rise.

It might take a little longer to get there, but he was sure the tractor would pull it out. It seemed to take forever to go the two kilometres down to the creek, and the rain got heavier when he was halfway there. As he came down the hill towards the camp area, he could see a light glowing in the small tent Violet had set up before his arrival.

Good, at least she was out of the rain.

She came out of the tent as he parked the tractor at the edge of the creek and he was pleased when she shone a large flashlight onto the stationery ute.

Joe frowned as she stared at the creek. "It must be raining in the hills. The creek's come up a bit already."

"I was hoping I was imagining that. I thought it was higher up the tyres," Violet said wiping her damp hair back from her eyes. "Will we have time?"

"Yep, as long as we get started now. If the water comes down fast it could push your car down the creek. Just in case, do you have insurance?"

She nodded. "I have insurance. That car cost me sixty thousand dollars, and I am not a happy camper," she said.

"I don't blame you. Are you right to steer while I drag it out?" When she nodded, Joe said, "Hop in now, no point getting any wetter."

Not to mention that the wetter her T-shirt got, the more it clung to her curves.

Violet hurried across to the ute, opened the door and climbed into the driver's side. Joe glanced over as he walked up the incline after securing the chain to the bar underneath the bull bar. He jumped in the tractor, and it started with a roar. She might be old, but she was sturdy and reliable.

"Knock it into neutral," he called out.

"It won't move," Violet called back.

He accelerated and moved forward slowly, and gradually he could feel the ute coming behind him. He kept the pressure on the accelerator, and it was only a few minutes before the ute was out of the creek. He kept going until they reached the top of the slight incline. He moved to the side of the road, turned the tractor off and climbed down.

"Thank you so much, Joe. I really appreciate it. Can I pay you for your trouble?" Violet had wound her window down, and he stood beside her, rain dripping off his hat.

"No, but there's one thing you can do for me."

Her eyes narrowed and he could see what she was thinking.

"Look, you're going to have to come with me tonight."

"Why?" Her face was closed.

"Because the creek is rising fast and if you leave your camp set up there, you'll be camped in the middle of the creek in an hour or so."

Her eyes widened and she opened the door and climbed out.

"Bloody hell,' she said. "I owe you big time, Joe. I'm sorry for what I was thinking."

"I'll help you get the tent down, and your sway in the back of the ute. Dismantle everything and throw it in the back of the ute. You can come back with me."

He watched Violet bite her lip, and he could see the thoughts churning in her head.

"Look, I live by myself, and so you feel at ease, once we get back to my place, we'll call the police station or my sister-in-law, who's the principal at the high school. They'll vouch for my character. I can understand you being hesitant, and I admire your caution."

"No, that's fine." Violet's now very wet shoulders relaxed. Joe didn't let his eyes stray any lower. "You've helped me, and I can see for myself that creek is coming up. I just appreciate your help." She smiled and the light of the torch caught the raindrops shimmering on her long dark eyelashes. "I would've really been up the creek without a paddle if you hadn't come along."

"It's all good. Come and we'll get your gear packed away. Have you got a rain jacket? I can give you my oilskin."

She shook her head and looked down ruefully. "Too late now."

They worked well together and soon her tent and swag were in the ute.

"I'll just throw some dirt on the fire, just in case," Violet said.

"You get in, I'll do that. It'll take us about twenty minutes for the tractor to pull you along to the house. I just hope it doesn't do too much damage to your car, towing it like that. The brakes will be heavier with the motor not on.'"

"I don't care if it does," she said as she opened the car door. "What's happened is the responsibility of the car manufacturer, and once the problem is diagnosed, I'll be fighting to get a refund or a new ute."

"Where did you buy it?"

"In a city."

Joe sensed that Violet didn't want to share too much about herself, and he could understand that. He wondered why she was travelling alone, and where she was going.

"Jump in, and we'll head home," he said as he hurried across to the last glowing embers of the fire. The rain began to pelt down.

Chapter 5
Violet

By the time they reached the farm a couple of kilometres along the road, the rain was bucketing down. The small roof on top of the tractor sheltered Joe to some extent, and even though he was wearing an oilskin, Violet was sure he was getting pretty wet.

She was wet, but safe and snug in the cab of the ute, gripping the wheel as the steering was hard with the motor not on, and keeping the ute on the road as the tractor pulled it along. As they had had feared it wouldn't go into neutral and the wheels weren't spinning. Her brand-new beauty was being skull dragged along a bumpy gravel road, probably shredding the tyres in the process. Despite being unsealed, the road wasn't in bad condition, but occasionally they hit a big pothole, and as they approached each one Joe would slow down a bit so she knew it was coming up.

It was pitch dark by the time they turned into an open gate and approached a farmhouse where a light shone from the back porch. Violet wondered if she was doing the right thing; Joe lived alone and she didn't know him. Her choices were limited: she could have stayed at the clearing and had her car washed into the creek and her campsite inundated with flood water, or she could stay with an unknown man in an isolated farmhouse. All the horror movies Violet had ever watched flickered through her head. She could always leave the car here and ask him to drive her into town.

"No, that would be unfair. There's no reason why I couldn't pitch my tent in his shed," she reasoned with herself. "The rain can't last all night, and I'd be dry."

Joe pulled up beside the shed she'd noticed and hopped off the tractor. Violet got out of the car and quickly followed Joe as he ran across to the back porch of the farmhouse.

"Well," he said. "They didn't forecast that storm. It was supposed to be a clear night. The rain seems to come out of the valley, and it can be pouring here with not a drop in town. We've been known to go for weeks without rain in town, but up here in the valley near the national park, we can get two or three inches in the same period of time."

"Good for the paddocks, I guess," Violet said.

Joe hesitated as he glanced at her and then turned away. "You're soaked. I'll grab you a towel, and I'll put the kettle on. I could do with a cuppa."

He was back quickly and handed her a soft towel.

"Thank you."

"Did you manage to eat your dinner before I came back?"

"Yes, I've eaten. Thank you." A thought struck her. "But you probably haven't. I feel terrible. I've dragged you out into the rain, and you got soaking wet, and you haven't even eaten."

"Don't worry about me," Joe reassured her, "I was painting and then I had a visitor. The day got away and I had a late lunch before I went out for a ride. I wasn't planning on much for dinner. Come in and sit at the table while I have a quick shower, but don't touch the walls. They're probably still tacky. And make yourself at home."

"Can I help? Can I make a pot of tea, or do

you use teabags or coffee?"

"Are you a tea or coffee drinker?"

Violet had spied the brand-new coffee machine on the benchtop in the corner of the kitchen. It was the same brand as the one she'd left behind. Her mouth watered at the thought of real coffee. She'd been living on instant since she'd started camping. The machine was plugged in and it looked like it was well-used.

"A real coffee would be good, if that's okay."

"So, you're a coffee addict too?" Joe grinned as he walked over and switched on the machine.

Violet nodded. "You?"

He opened the cupboard above the coffee machine, careful not to touch the walls with the cupboard door. She smiled as she saw an array of coffee pods in all different colours.

"Come and have a browse and decide what you want while the water heats up in it, and I'll be back in a minute."

Violet looked around the kitchen as she waited. After she had chosen her favourite Arpeggio coffee pod, she let her eyes wander around the room. The benchtops and cupboards were obviously new, and she could still smell the paint in the room. There was a gap beneath the sink where she assumed where a dishwasher would eventually go.

Considering the room was in the middle of a renovation, it was remarkably dust free and tidy. She was fast picking up the impression that Joe was an organised and competent guy.

"He must think I'm an absolute twit," she thought, rolling her eyes. "Camped next to a creek that was going to get flooded, the car broken down in the middle of the crossing. What else can go wrong?"

Joe came out and smiled when he saw the coffee pod on the benchtop. He reached up and pulled down two mugs. "Do you have milk in yours?"

Violet replied, "Yes, please. I waited to see which one you would like. You have a great selection."

"Mine is the same as you've picked out. I love the woody flavour of Arpeggio."

"Ah, a true afficionado."

'The only coffee that beats home is at the Cyprus Café in town. I've picked Nic's brains over how he brews their coffee, but he always taps his nose and tells me it's a Greek secret. I'll have to take you there when we take your ute to town."

"My favourite—" Violet hesitated. She'd been about to say her favourite coffee shop was in the Valley in Brisbane, but she caught herself just in time. She didn't want anyone to know anything about her. She stared again. "That's my favourite type of coffee too."

"Would you like a toasted sandwich with it?" Joe asked. "I'm going to have one."

Violet declined. "No, thank you. I had enough dinner."

Joe went to the fridge and took out a loaf of bread, some ham slices, tomato, and a packet of grated cheese. Within minutes, he had a toastie bubbling away in a flat-topped sandwich maker, and then he turned to the coffee machine.

There was a companiable silence as they sat at the table together. Joe was eating his toastie, Violet was thinking, wondering if she could get the ute sorted tomorrow.

Joe's voice broke into her thoughts. "Have a biscuit. There's plenty there."

"Thank you." Violet reached for one of the homemade ANZAC biscuits Joe had put on a plate in front of them.

"Did you bake these?" she asked after taking a bite. "They're good."

Joe chuckled. "No. I bought them at the CWA cake stall."

"I don't bake," Violet said. "I eat too many biscuits if I do. Is baking another of your skills?" She looked around the kitchen, admiring his work.

"Skills? I don't have many of them." Joe frowned. "Not much education, no qualifications. I'm just a builder's labourer." His face reddened slightly

Violet disagreed. "I've known you a little bit over an hour and I already know you can renovate a house, drive a tractor, ride a horse, run a farm and rescue stranded women. I was sure baking would be part of your repertoire."

He grinned at her teasing tone. "No, Ryan, my brother sent me into town one day this week to get some new nails for a job we're working on, and there was a CWA stall in the main street. As soon as I spotted Florrie Miller's Anzacs, I bought up the lot and took them back to Ryan, and we had quite a feed for smoko. I brought the rest home, filled the biscuit barrel and put the rest in the freezer. I'm set for biscuits until the other side of Christmas."

"You'll have to learn how to make them if you love them that much."

His laugh was hearty and brought a smile to Violet's face. As Joe held her gaze steadily, the laughter lines in his tanned face deepened, and she found it hard to look away. They were eyes a girl could get lost in.

"No, cooking is sure not my forte," he said. "Toasted sandwiches just about do it. Maybe a steak on the barbie when it's not raining."

"What about veggies?"

"Do hot chips count as veggies?" Joe was still holding her eyes with his.

"No," Violet said.

"Okay. I sometimes have a salad roll for lunch. Thea at the Cyprus Café makes a good one. Lots of green stuff on it."

"Good, I won't worry about my rescuer suffering from scurvy once I've left town."

"Scurvy? What's that?"

"That's what sailors used to get from not eating enough fresh fruit and veggies."

"I eat lots of fruit."

'Good, I won't worry about you. I can focus

on worrying about my damn ute." Violet stood and went over to the window and looked out at said ute. Big fat raindrops bounced in the puddles that had formed in the driveway since they had arrived.

"Would you like another coffee?" Joe asked.

"No thanks. That was lovely. And so was the Anzac."

"Come on, we'll go into the living room and call Jac from the landline. The mobile service is pretty dodgy."

"Yeah, I noticed that. I'm supposed to call my sister and report in tonight."

"Feel free to use the landline after we've made a call," Joe said as they walked to the living room up the hallway near what she assumed was the front door.

Violet shook her head as she followed him into the room where a huge Christmas tree sat in the corner. "No, it's fine. I'll call her from town tomorrow. And look, you don't have to ring anyone. I'm fine. I appreciate you looking after me."

He shook his head. "Haven't you read Hansel and Gretel? Remember the kind old lady?"

"I don't see the connection."

"All she was going to do was fatten the kids up. I don't want you lying there all night worrying that I have wicked intentions. I'd feel happier if you talk to Jac."

"Okay, if it makes you feel better. Go ahead."

"Good." Joe dialled the number, and within seconds, he said, "Hey Ryan, it's Joe. Can I talk to Jac, please?" He listened for a moment. "Yes, all good tomorrow. I've got a bit of a favour to ask Jac. See you tomorrow, bro."

Violet watched Joe as he spoke. When he glanced over and caught her staring at him her cheeks heated and she looked down.

"Hi Jac. I played the shining white knight on old Sam today and rescued a young lady who was broken down in my creek. She'd set up camp, but I brought her and her ute back here behind the tractor because of the rain."

He paused and listened for a moment. "Isn't it raining in town?"

His sister-in-law had obviously commented on the weather.

"Well, it's teeming down here, but anyway, listen, I'll put you onto Violet. She's passing through, her car's not looking good, and I've offered for her to sleep on the side veranda. We need to get her car into Fred's Garage."

Another pause.

"That's right. She did look a bit hesitant." He met Violet's eyes across the telephone, and she smiled to reassure him that she no longer had any doubts about staying at the farm. "Sensible young woman. I wanted to get some character references. Are you happy to say something nice about me, Jack?"

His sister-in-law obviously said something humorous because Joe burst out laughing.

"Now that's not nice. Okay I know you were joking."

Joe smiled and handed the phone over. "My sister-in-law's name is Jaclyn, but we call her Jac for short."

Violet took the phone; it had been a long time since she used a landline. They depended on mobiles at the business in Brisbane, too.

"Hello, Jac this is Violet Valentine speaking," she said softly.

"Hello, Violet, I'm Jaclyn Rossiter. I'm Joe's sister-in-law. I believe you've had some car trouble."

"Yes, I have. I'm not impressed. It's a brand-new ute, setting off on the trip, and it's hardly got me across the border."

"Not good at all. Anyway, even though I teased Joe, I can certainly give you an excellent character reference. He's a great guy and I'm not saying that because I'm married to his brother. Joe is a true gentleman, and you're quite safe in the house with him tonight."

"Thank you, I had already decided that when I met Joe, but he insisted that we call you."

"Well, there you go; that's Joe. You couldn't have chosen a much better spot to break down. And you can never be too careful, even in a little country town like Bindarra Creek. Will you still be there tomorrow?" she asked.

"Oh no, I'll need to get into town."

"There'll be no mechanic on duty tomorrow, and the NRMA can take hours to get here from Tamworth. You're probably best to wait until Monday. Ryan has a car trailer. I'll get him to talk to Joe. We can easily bring it over tomorrow."

"Thank you, I appreciate it." Violet frowned as first her thoughts, and then her stomach churned. She'd have to find somewhere to stay. Jaclyn spoke before she could say any more.

"Listen, I might be organising you. Joe and I are the world's biggest organisers, and my husband is rolling his eyes right now. Why don't you stay for lunch tomorrow, and you can come back to town with us? We can drop you at the motel or the caravan park cabins or whatever suits you while you get your car sorted."

"That's very kind of you; it would save Joe a trip into town in the morning. I suppose he'll be getting lunch cooked."

Jaclyn's laughter tinkled down the phone. "Oh no, hasn't he told you yet? Joe doesn't cook."

"Actually, we've just had a discussion about Anzac biscuits, toasted sandwiches, and vegetables."

"He's warmed to you if he's telling you about his one lacking talent. Joe does not cook. So, I'm bringing lunch out tomorrow because he wanted to have the first Christmas in his new house as a family and we won't be here Christmas Day. My sweet husband surprised me with a trip to the Cook Islands. Poor Joe is going to be all by himself on Christmas Day. So, tomorrow is our Christmas."

"I really feel like I'm intruding. If it's a nice day, I can wander around and set up camp somewhere on the property and mind my own business until you're ready to take me back into town."

"No, of course we wouldn't do that; that's not how we work in Bindarra Creek. I'm sure Joe will agree with me. Can you put him back on for me, please, Violet? I look forward to meeting you tomorrow."

Joe took the phone from Violet and held her gaze steadily as he listened to his sister-in-law. He nodded a few times and then finished the call.

"Sounds good to me," he said to Violet "Looks like we're six for lunch tomorrow."

"And I believe you're not cooking," she said with a tentative smile.

"Jac's been preparing the full-on Christmas feast. All I have to do is turn the oven on." His grin sent a sweet little shimmer down her back.

How lucky had she been to break down near such a nice guy's farm?

Chapter 6
Violet

Violet slept surprisingly well. Joe had insisted that she sleep on the veranda sleepout. She made sure she was up, had a wash, and was dressed early the next morning. She didn't want to look like someone who was going to stay in bed while her host did the work.

Even though she was up just after sunrise, Joe had beaten her. He was sitting on the back steps, waiting to hear her stir inside when she walked to the back door.

"You're up bright and early for someone who was rescued during the night," he said. "You should've made yourself a coffee before you came out."

"Oh, I didn't want to impose."

"Well, I'm dying for one, and a piece of toast? Or would you like some cereal?"

"I'm impressed this motel room includes breakfast."

"And the fancy lunch we're about to have."

Violet made the coffee while Joe put some bread in the toaster. "What would you like on your toast? Jam, peanut butter, or Vegemite.

She pulled a face. "Ergh, not peanut butter."

"It's the food of the gods," he said holding the jar up. "So I guess I won't put it on both pieces of toast."

"Vegemite will do me nicely, thank you."

Joe pulled a similar face to the one she'd just pulled. "Yuck. I only have Vegemite in the fridge for Georgia. She loves it."

"She has good taste. Can you call yourself an Aussie bushman?" she said. "Vegemite should be the staple diet for you."

The atmosphere in the kitchen was light and warm; Violet had managed to leave the worry of her car; worrying would achieve nothing.

"If I have to spend a few days in Bindarra Creek while the car is fixed, so be it," she'd told herself when she woke up in the strange house.

They sat on the back steps sipping their coffee and munching toast in the early morning sun before the heat of the day began to build. It was a brilliant day and the deep blue sky was clear.

"Joe? Could I ask you another favour?"

Violet asked when she'd finished her toast. "My phone is still out of service, even here at your farmhouse. Who are you with?"

"Telstra," he said. "But even that service drops out some days. That's why I still have the landline," he said.

"I was wondering if I could make a phone call and sort out some accommodation in town for tonight and tomorrow night? I imagine it's going to take them at least a day to fix the car."

He looked over at her, a frown creasing his brow. "Do you want the good news or the bad news?"

"Hit me with the bad news," she said.

"I'd say it's going to take a bit longer than a day or two."

"Do you think so?" Violet asked.

"A week maybe." Joe shrugged and held her gaze as if to soften the blow. "At best, I'd say."

"Surely not? Isn't there a mechanic in town?"

"Yes, Dale Highgrove who took over Fred's Garage has a really good reputation. I'm no mechanic but I know enough to guess you're going to be up for a new gearbox."

"It's under warranty, so be it."

"The problem is, you're probably used to being in the city and getting things quickly. To get a new gearbox for a car out here, even when it's not heading for Christmas holidays, can often take up to a month. If not longer."

"A month?" Violet almost choked on the coffee that she had just sipped as she squeaked the words out. She swallowed quickly. "Really? But it can't be a month. I've got to go to—" She took a deep breath. "I have a job interview in the Hunter Valley the week after next, and I was mooching around the west of New South Wales filling in time on the way."

"We'll wait and see what Dale at the garage says, but don't be surprised when he says that you might be spending some time in Bindarra Creek."

"Well, that's what I was going to check— what the accommodation situation is like in town. Is there a motel?"

"Yes, a motel and cabins at the caravan park, and there are a couple of guest houses and Air BNBs in town. So, you shouldn't have any trouble."

"Can you recommend any of them?"

"Well, I'd recommend Edwina Lette's Fig

Tree Lodge. It's pretty good, I hear. Nice old double-storey house. Jac lived there for a while when she first came to town. I'm not sure if it's open at the moment, but I can give you the number."

"Thanks. What about the caravan park and the motel?" Violet shook her head. "Look, don't worry, when I get into town, I assume I'll have phone service and I can look them up."

"You might as well call from here. The local directory is near the phone. You should find them all in there."

"Thank you. I'll leave it until after 8:30 when they will open," Violet said.

"Maybe." Joe looked at her again over the coffee cup. "This is Bindarra Creek, and it is Sunday. You might have to leave a message, and they'll get back to you."

"Oh dear, I'm not used to this. I'm used to the pace of the city, where everything is open twenty-four-seven." She forced a smile. "Although it is a pleasant pace of life, I guess."

"It is a very good way to live." Joe leaned back on the brick wall at the side of the landing. "I enjoyed the big town life in my twenties. You know the sort of thing? Friday night at the pub, Saturday at the local race meet, and then Sundays back at the pub to prepare for the week ahead."

Violet nodded, even though it described a very different life to her twenties. She'd studied, worked three jobs, and then gone straight to work at the thoroughbred stud when she'd graduated.

"I wasted a lot of money back then," Joe added. "I spent most of my time between shearing jobs, socialising not in the city, but in the big country towns: Parkes, Forbes, Dubbo, and the like. Then when Ryan moved here with his job, I came back to the district and did most of my shearing around here."

"You grew up here?"

"No. I meant I came back here because I'd visited him when he first bought *Rossiter's Run*. Before he met up with Jac again. That's the name of their property. Ryan and I grew up down at Werris Creek. Then when Mum ditched our stepdad, we moved to Coonabarabran. I travelled around for a few years and Ryan worked in Sydney for a while, and then came to the western district as a building inspector for the Education Department." He looked a bit shamefaced. "I was a bit of a lad in my twenties. I didn't even go to TAFE."

"Sounds like you had fun though." Her voice was wistful. *Fun.* That was something that Violet hadn't had much of.

"Yep, I was shearing and going around from town to town, staying in dongas and bunking in sheds and I didn't want to settle. It's only when I came back here when Ryan and Jac got married that I thought about settling down. I started working with Ryan and Grant, and I finally got in the swing of things. Saved a bit of money, and started to think about the long term here. It's a great little town, and when this property came up, I thought, why not?"

"It sounds idyllic." No cars, no traffic, and just peace and quiet. Violet had enjoyed this unexpected stop so far, even though she hadn't been into town, Joe had made it sound attractive.

"It's the best thing I ever did. And it's the happiest I've been for a long time," he said, looking at her critically. "What about you, Violet? What's your story?"

"My story?" She lowered her eyes while Joe waited. "Pretty boring actually. This is the sort of place I could imagine living. I've always worked in the city. This is heaven."

After a minute Joe obviously realised she wasn't going to share her life story, and he stood. "I'd better go and feed the animals. Make yourself at home."

Chapter 7
Violet

Violet followed Joe into the kitchen and when he went to rinse his cup and plate, she touched his arm.

"Leave that. I'll do the dishes and tidy up, It's the least I can do."

"No dishwasher," he said.

She smiled. "I don't mind washing up a couple of cups and plates. You've been so kind to invite me to stay for lunch. Is there anything I can do?"

"No, Jac'll bring it all."

"What about the Christmas table? What do you do? Do you sit outside or in the dining room?"

"We'll eat in the dining room, the big room on the other side of the living room where you saw the Christmas tree last night."

"Because it's cooler inside?"

"No, because it's such a great room. There's a big table and eight timber chairs in there that belonged to the original owners. Hand-hewn timber, it's a beautiful piece. It's too heavy to move, so each time the house is sold the dining room setting stays with it. They must have built it in the room about a hundred years ago. To be honest that was what really swayed me. I was looking at a couple of other properties. One house had already been renovated, but I loved the dining room setting here, and I figured I could do up the place how I wanted."

"Has the farm sold often?"

"Not really. I'm only the third owner. The original family had it for about four generations. The old couple passed on about five years ago. Sadly, they didn't have any children, so it was bought by a young couple from the city who decided after a couple of years that the rural lifestyle wasn't what they thought it would be. Suits me. I'll be staying here."

"Starting your own line of sheep farmers one day," Violet said.

"Who knows," Joe said with a grin, "You can't discount anything in the future."

Violet shooed him out of the kitchen. "Right, you go and do your chores and I'll get the dining room table set once I clean the kitchen." She tipped her head to the side. "Hang on, do you have tablecloths and things like that?"

"You're in for a surprise. As well as the dining setting, the linen cupboards in the back of the house were left full of the old couple's stuff. I guess there was nowhere else for it to go, and the house was sold as it was. The next owners left it all there. I've got no idea what's in there." He gave her a mischievous grin. "Probably mice and cockroaches."

"I can cope with that. I lived in some pretty ordinary digs when I was at uni."

"Don't go to too much trouble. The timber table is good enough to just set the cutlery on without a cloth. I did buy some bonbons for Georgia and a couple of Christmas ornament things. They're in the white paper bag under the Christmas tree."

"Would you mind if I had a poke around those linen cupboards?"

"Knock yourself out. I'll be out in the paddock for an hour or two. And please, make yourself at home. If you want another coffee, help yourself. Use the phone when you want to, and if you're happy to set the table, that sounds good to me."

"One more thing," she asked. "Is it okay if I have a shower and wash my hair?"

"Of course, you can. I should've offered and showed you where the loo and the basin were last night, but I guess you found them okay. There's actually two bathrooms, the main bathroom near the porch, and there's a smaller one that I use off my bedroom. I'll grab some towels."

"No, don't worry," she said. "I've got my own towel. Everything I need is in the ute. I'm set up for camping, remember. I just need to have a quick shower." She refrained from saying that all her worldly possessions were in the back of the ute.

Except for her coffee machine which she'd left at Brian's.

"Help yourself. Like I said, Violet, please make yourself at home." His grin set a zing running through her. He held her gaze again and she wondered if he'd felt it too.

"Listen, Joe. I'm going to buy you a carton of beer when I leave here tomorrow—not just that one beer I said I owed you."

"You don't need to do that. It's been great to have company this morning."

With another grin, Joe pulled on his work boots and disappeared out the back door. He was uncomplicated and his upbeat nature added to the calm that had stolen over Violet as soon as she'd arrived here—despite her car issues. She'd get it fixed eventually.

Once she'd done the dishes, and given the kitchen a good wipe over, she headed out to the ute in her still mud-stained shorts and T-shirt. She'd slept in her underwear, and pulled on yesterday's clothes before she'd come out to the kitchen this morning. Her ute was still hooked up to the tractor.

"I am gradually liking you less and less," she muttered to the vehicle when the remote didn't release the door lock on the first click. She pressed the button again, and panic was about to set in as she looked through the closed window at her bags on the passenger seat. That would be nice, sitting at a Christmas lunch in her muddy shorts and T-shirt.

Relief was sweet as the door unlocked with an extra loud click on the third attempt.

Pulling out her kit bag, Violet took out some clean undies, another pair of shorts, and a T-shirt. In the corner of her bag, she had a light jersey dress rolled into a ball. She'd hang it up in the shower to get the creases out and change before lunch. It was going to be a hot day, and a dress would be more appropriate for the family lunch she'd been invited to.

Still feeling as though she was intruding, she had a super-fast, but deliciously hot shower, quickly washing and rinsing her hair. She'd bought in her small toiletries bag last night and left it on the end of the bed on the porch. She'd slept surprisingly well in that bed last night, and for the first time in weeks, she hadn't dreamed about Brian, or about trying to escape from a locked room.

Her dreams over the past months had truly reflected her state of mind, and now she had escaped, she could move on. Being out of that toxic workplace was the best thing, and the healing had begun already.

Joe was the total opposite of Brian; easy to get on with, accommodating, and an all-round nice guy. Brian had been demanding and negative and had seemed to get his kicks out of bringing her down. The couple of times she tried to talk to him about it, he'd turned it around to be her fault, and she'd lost even more self-esteem.

And what have you learned, she asked herself.

Never get involved with anyone in the workplace, she told herself firmly. Maybe not get involved with anyone until she really knew them well.

Violet hummed as she found a broom on the back landing, and swept out the kitchen. Once she'd stripped her bed on the porch and folded up the sheets, she put them in the laundry at the back of the kitchen. She put her muddy clothes back in the car, and put her makeup bag in the bathroom, with the dress she'd steamed as she showered, ready to change before Joe's family arrived.

She still felt awkward about the situation, but she had to make the best of it, and she could help by setting a nice table.

If she could find a tablecloth. She grinned. If not, she'd do what he suggested.

Surprise filled her when she found the linen press in the back of the house. Opening the door carefully, she expected to see cockroaches and mice droppings, but the sweet smell of lavender greeted her. The shelves were full of linen sheets and embroidered pillow cases; there were even crocheted doilies like her Gran used to edge in ecru crochet cotton. She smiled as she remembered Gran trying to teach her to crochet when she'd been a little girl, but the skill had never interested her. Violet had been a tomboy and had much preferred to be outside with Pop and the horses.

That's where her love of the animals had come from. Her eyes widened as she poked around the cupboard; there were some beautiful pieces in here. How sad that there hadn't been a family for it to be passed down to.

Some of the delicate pieces looked as though they should be in a museum or gallery; she wondered if Joe had even looked in the cupboard. It was a far cry from the mice and cockroaches he'd expected. She crouched down and smiled when she spotted some placemats with a red and green crocheted edge. Beside them were some old-fashioned Christmas decorations and some fat red and green candles.

She wondered sadly who the childless couple had celebrated Christmas with. Blinking back a tear as she remembered her childhood Christmases at her grandparents' house with all the cousins.

Those ties had long gone as they'd all grown up and gone out into the world. They had been so close as kids, and now they barely communicated.

Forcing away her maudlin mood, Violet went into the living room, collected the bon bons and the ornaments that Joe had bought, and then she set to work. The huge timber table was superb and when she found some beeswax in the laundry, Violet polished the table until it shone. Deciding to forgo a table cloth, she quickly aired the crochet-edged placemats and set the table. At one stage, she actually found herself singing Christmas carols under her breath, and she smiled.

Once the table was set, she stood back and was very happy with the result. That was certainly an unexpected contribution to the lunch.

Now that the kitchen was clean and the table was set, she went to the living room and picked up the telephone. As promised, Joe, in his easy organised way, had left the directory. She could have done with him in the office at the stud. He followed through with his promises.

There was a small ad for Fig Tree Lodge in the directory and it looked lovely. The whole view of the house was obscured by the large Moreton Bay Fig in the centre of the lawn; there was just a small glimpse of white wrought iron lace edging a top veranda.

It was the first place she called; she could imagine relaxing on that veranda.

"Good morning, Fig Tree Lodge, Edwina Lette speaking."

"Oh, good morning. My name is Violet Valentine, and I'm passing through town, and I know it's very short notice, but I'm hoping that you'll be able to accommodate me in a single room for the next four or five nights." Violet crossed her fingers, hoping that was the maximum the stay would be.

"Oh, I'm very sorry, my dear. I'm totally booked out until the end of January."

"Oh, okay. Well, thank you for your time."

"My pleasure."

She hung up and dialled the motel number. She didn't really fancy staying in a cabin in the caravan park, even though she was used to swagging it and tenting.

The motel rang out as Joe had suggested, so

she left a message on the phone and asked if they could accommodate her from tonight for five nights, leaving her number.

Her last call was the caravan park. The call picked up on the first ring.

"Oh, hello," she said. "I was hoping you could accommodate me in a cabin for the next five nights."

The response was a laugh. "No chance at all, love. We've got a group of veteran motorbike enthusiasts here for the next week, and everything in town is full. We've got nothing. No cabins, no sites powered or unpowered."

"Thank you," Violet said. Not even an unpowered site in town.

What the heck am I going to do?

As she walked slowly out to the porch a red sedan towing a car trailer turned into the driveway; it must be Joe's family and he wasn't back yet. She quickly hurried to the sleepout and changed into her dress, then ran a brush through her now-dry hair, and rubbed some pink lip gloss onto her lips. Walking to the back door, nerves skittered in; she wasn't good with strangers.

Violet was about to have an early Christmas

meal with strangers.

Chapter 8
Joe

Joe cleaned up the mess that Molly had made in her pen through the night and then he topped up her water, filled her bowl with kibble, and sat on the concrete steps leading up to the dog pen. Molly came over and sniffed around him. Eventually, she sat down beside him and rested her silky head on his lap.

"When are you going to have those pups, Molly?" he murmured. His fingers played with her silky ears as he thought about meeting Violet the night before.

It was funny; what he'd been thinking about when Holly delivered the basket yesterday, but when he'd looked at Violet, the strangest feeling had shot through him, a sort of sense of meeting his fate. A warm tingling had settled in his chest and his belly, and he'd found it hard to look away. That had never happened to him before with any of the women he'd met over the past few years as he'd travelled around, and then settled in Bindarra Creek.

Maybe because it was a reaction to her tight

T-shirt over a fit and toned body. He wondered if that was what it was all about. He had laid awake for a long time last night after he'd gone to bed, thinking of her in the spare bed out in the sleepout.

Maybe it was because he was worried about her; she'd seemed pretty stressed about the car issues at first, but had relaxed gradually last night. Her company had been fun, and he'd enjoyed their conversation, not that she'd talked much about herself.

At first, he'd been surprised to see a single woman driving a big vehicle like that, and camping out in the scrub. Granted, that was the sort of woman that he'd dreamed about a couple of years ago when he was actively thinking of settling down; the sort of person he'd like to have a relationship with. But he'd never met anyone like that. All the girls he'd met just wanted to go to the pub or to the movies or to the club to dance and watch a show. That sort of things didn't appeal to him at all. He was an outdoors guy, and now that he had his own place, he was turning into a real homebody and didn't need to go out. He certainly had plenty of things here to fill his days and nights.

But it certainly been good to have company last night.

Joe pushed himself to his feet. "Come on, Molly. We'll go for a wander, and check those sheep down in the back corner." The pump at the creek had kicked in overnight, and the sheep troughs were full of clear water. The sheep were over in the far back paddock, and the fences were secure. He'd spent a lot of time working on them in the last couple of weeks, in between working for Grant and Ryan, because once he got his first breeders in, he didn't want any foxes or dingoes to get to them. He'd built a solid fence and enclosed the sheep he already had into a half-acre secure paddock.

Joe walked along, checking that the fence was intact and then checked the irrigation pipes in the next paddock. Considering he'd only been here a few months he was pretty damn proud of what he'd done so far. Once he got the house renovated, he could start thinking about building himself a big shed and getting some farm equipment. But that was a fair way down the track because he had to save some money first. He'd spent all of his savings on the deposit for the house, and with Ryan going on holidays there wasn't much work coming in on the building side of things for the next month. Grant had said that the landscaping work would ease off over Christmas and into the New Year. He was taking Cathy and the kids down to the coast for a couple of weeks to see the kids' grandparents.

Joe had thought about calling in at the pub and seeing if they needed extra bar staff over the break. When he'd lived in Tamworth between contracts, he got his RSA, and he was quite handy behind the bar. He made a mental note to do that when he went into town tomorrow.

As he and Molly headed back to the house paddock, the sound of an approaching car caught his attention. Jaclyn's red sedan turned off the dirt road into his driveway.

Joe glanced at his watch; he'd been fiddling around outside for longer than he'd thought. He'd intended having a shower before they arrived. He stopped at the tap at the back of the old shed, washed his hands, sluiced his face with the cool water, and then ran his fingers through his hair. At least he had decent jeans and a T-shirt on, not his old work clothes.

And why did you dress like that this morning, he asked himself. Did it have anything to do with your pretty guest?

He headed across to the driveway where Ryan had pulled the car up beside Violet's ute. He looked across at the house; Violet was standing inside the back door. For a moment he thought about going over and bringing her outside to meet them, but instead he detoured to the car and walked around to the passenger side as Jaclyn got out. There'd be time enough for introductions once they were inside.

"Hey, Jac, it sounds funny even though it's only the first week in December, but Merry Christmas."

"Merry Christmas to you too, Joe." Jaclyn put her hands on his shoulders and stood on her tiptoes to kiss his cheek.

Ryan came around the front of the car carrying Georgia. He held out one arm and gave his brother a hug. "Merry Christmas, bro. Now tell me, who is this new person you've got staying in your place? Jaclyn was talking about someone breaking down, but she didn't know the full story. She didn't listen properly last night."

"Only because you kept interrupting and wanting to know what Violet was saying," Jaclyn said with a patient smile.

"She was travelling through to Bindarra Creek and broke down in the creek."

Ryan looked over at the ute that was still hooked to the tractor with the length of chain.

"Looks like a brand-new vehicle."

"It is," Joe said. "I'll help you unpack and you can meet her, and she can tell you all about it."

Maybe Violet might be more forthcoming about where she'd come from now that Jac and Ryan were here. All that he'd picked up so far was that she'd been to uni, lived in the city, and had a job interview in the Hunter Valley next week.

Chapter 9
Joe

As Joe walked around to the back of the sedan, Georgia started squealing and held her arms out to him, pushing away from her father.

"Happy Christmas, kiddo," Joe said, taking his little niece and pressing his face against her sweet-smelling cheeks. "How's my little girl?"

"Jo Jo," she said, followed by a gurgle of sounds that could have meant anything.

"You smell like strawberries, Georgie-girl."

"That's why we were late, Joe," Jaclyn said. "We would have been here half an hour ago, but I made the mistake of giving Georgia her Sippy cup after I put her in the Christmas dress I bought specially for her to wear today."

"A very pretty dress," Joe said.

"It was, before she tipped the drink all down the front. I had to take it off, sponge it down, and throw it in the clothes dryer for fifteen minutes. She's probably still got strawberry milk on her skin."

"Thus, our late, but sweet-smelling arrival." His brother grinned. "Wait until you get married, Joe; you've got all of this ahead of you."

Joe pulled a face. "I have to find someone to marry first; you got the best girl in Bindarra Creek."

"And I got the best brother-in-law in town." Jac patted Joe playfully on the shoulder as she walked around to the back of the car. "Can you unhook the car trailer and open the boot, please, love?" she said to Ryan.

Joe quickly unhooked the trailer and the boot popped open, and Ryan leaned in, taking out a couple of green Woolies bags.

"I'll take this in first, and then I'll come back for the stuff that's in the esky," he said.

"I'll get the pavlova," Jaclyn said

"I've got a spare hand." Joe sat Georgia on his hip. "I can bring the esky if you like."

"Sure?" Ryan asked as he reached for a third green grocery bag.

Joe rolled his eyes. "Not a very heavy esky; not a problem at all."

Once the boot was empty, the convoy of the three adults and one child made their way to the back of Joe's house.

Ryan looked around as they crossed the yard. "You've done a lot of work since we were last here."

"Yep, weekends are for working on the place. Wait until we're inside and you see the house. I've picked up a lot about renos and landscaping since I gave away shearing."

"It's the good teacher you've had." Ryan chuckled.

Violet wasn't at the door as Joe put the esky down and held the screen door opened for Ryan and Jaclyn to walk in and put the bags on the kitchen bench. He handed Georgia over and turned back for the esky.

As he came back into the kitchen, Jaclyn and Violet were shaking hands. He put the esky down as they introduced themselves.

"Hello," Jaclyn was saying. "You must be Violet."

"Yes, I am, and you must be Jaclyn," Violet said with a smile. She sent Joe a tentative glance, seeking reassurance.

Joe smiled back and walked to stand beside her. "Violet, meet Georgia, my very clever niece who obviously takes after her uncle. She's been calling me Jo Jo ever since she started talking last month. And this is my big brother, Ryan."

"Hello, Ryan." Violet turned back to Jaclyn after shaking Ryan's hand. "Thanks so much for inviting me today. I really feel as though I've gate-crashed a family do."

'Not at all, Violet. We wouldn't have asked you if we hadn't wanted to."

"Thank you. Now tell me how I can help in the kitchen. I believe you're cooking, Jaclyn?"

"Once we get this stuff in the fridge, I'll put the meat in the oven to heat it through. It's already cooked and sliced. Then I just have to make the gravy and put the baked vegies in the air fryer to warm them up." She turned to Ryan. "You did put the air fryer in, didn't you, Ryan?"

"Oops." His brother looked sheepish.

"Will the microwave do? There's a new one in the kitchen."

"It will," Jaclyn said.

"Good," Joe said. "Now come on, we're going to the living room, and Georgia can see my Christmas tree."

Once the cold stuff was in the fridge, they all followed Joe down the hall.

"I'm impressed," Ryan said. "Did Violet help you?"

"The beautiful Christmas tree was here when I arrived," Violet went to say more, but stopped.

"I did it all, but Holly David did help me straighten the star yesterday." Joe glanced at Violet, sensing that she had wanted to say something. "Come on. Let's sit down. The table's already set for lunch, thanks to Violet, so we can relax and have a drink."

Violet's cheeks went a pretty pink and her voice was soft. "Did you see it, Joe?"

"Not yet, did you find a tablecloth?"

"You'll see." Her smile was sweet; even when she'd had good reason to be stressed last night with her car breaking down and being towed behind his tractor up and down hills and through potholes in the rain, she remained calm and sensible, and that fuelled his attraction.

"Who'd like a drink?" Ryan asked.

"Of course we'd like a Christmas drink, even though it's only the first week in December," Jaclyn said.

Ryan stood and handed Georgia over to Jaclyn. "There's a six-pack in the esky, and there's a bottle of champagne there for the girls if they'd like that."

Violet's cheeks pinked again, and Joe wondered whether she was still feeling awkward about being included in their family Christmas celebration. A glass of champagne might help her relax

"Would you like a glass of champagne, Violet? Or a beer?" he asked.

She nodded. "Champagne, if that's okay."

"Of course it's okay. You've been invited to a Christmas dinner, and I want you to feel totally comfortable. Champagne will break the ice."

"It is better than sitting out in the bush in my broken-down ute."

Ryan brought two beers and a bottle of champagne from the kitchen.

"Uh oh," Joe frowned. "You didn't think to bring glasses, did you, Jac?"

His sister-in-law shook her head. "No."

"I've only got Vegemite glasses."

Violet's eyes held his and they both smiled.

Jaclyn looked at them both curiously and then glanced at Ryan.

"Give me a minute," Violet said.

Joe watched as she left the room and then felt Jac's eyes on him. She smiled and raised her eyebrows.

A minute later, Violet returned with two crystal flutes. "I found these in the mouse cupboard," she said. Her cheeks pinked again, and when her tongue slipped out and she licked her lips, Joe had a sudden urge to kiss her.

"The mouse cupboard?" he repeated slowly, trying to compose himself.

"It's okay, I've washed them. It was actually a treasure trove. You'll see when lunch is ready." She gave him a cheeky smile and put the two glasses on the table.

Ryan opened the champagne with a pop, and poured the frothing liquid into the flutes.

Joe lifted his glass and held Violet's eyes with his. "To new beginnings."

"Jo Jo," his niece squealed and he dragged his eyes from Violet's as the moment was interrupted.

Chapter 9
Violet

Lunch was a happy affair and Violet gradually relaxed and began to enjoy herself. She was ridiculously aware of Joe, more so than when it had just been the two of them, last night and this morning.

Joe had been impressed when they entered the huge dining room. Not only was the table set with a red and white table runner showing off the highly polished surface, but the red candles had made a simple centrepiece. The green candles took pride of place on the mantlepiece with some silver tinsel looped gracefully between them. The bonbons finished off the table nicely.

"Wow, thanks, Violet," Joe said. "You've done an amazing job. Whoever would have guessed all that was in the cupboard."

Violet sat back sipping her glass of bubbles as Joe explained.

"Violet asked me how she could help today,

and I suggested setting the table." He reached across the table and lightly touched her hand. "Thank you very much. You've turned my place into a home today."

"Well, I think you already have a very lovely home now, and it'll be even more beautiful when you finish it."

"You'll have to come and visit in a year or so when it's all done."

"I'll hold you to that," she said. She jumped as Georgia clapped her hands with a squeal and Violet turned to Jaclyn. "How old is Georgia?" she asked.

"She'll be one on New Year's Day," Jaclyn said. "We'll be home from our holiday just in time for her first birthday party. I'd love you to come if you're still in Bindarra Creek."

"Oh. I'll be long gone by then," Violet said. "I hope, anyway."

"And then it's only a few weeks until I go back to work full-time after the school holidays. I honestly don't know how I'm going to leave her."

"Have you got someone to mind her?" Joe asked.

"Yes, Cleo said she's happy to have her full

time now that Benny's off to pre-school, and Charlotte is two."

Violet picked up her glass of champagne and sipped slowly. The last thing she wanted was her head to get fuzzy and her tongue to get loose.

So far, the Rossiters hadn't asked her where she was going, or what she should've been doing for Christmas, or what she did for a living. But she was sure that would come as the afternoon progressed.

Sure enough, only a minute later, after Jaclyn had set Georgia on her lap and was giving her a drink from her Sippy cup, she turned to Violet. "So, you're heading south, Violet? Joe said you had major car troubles."

"Yes, I am. And yes, the car has been a pain. Remember how you mentioned about getting a lift into town with you this afternoon? I don't know what I'm going to do because everywhere is booked out. I called the Fig Tree Lodge that you suggested, Joe, but it's booked out, the caravan park has some vintage bikers there and no vacancies, and the motel is full." She pulled a face. "I guess, I'll have to find a camp somewhere while my car problem is sorted."

Ryan nodded. "Yes, I saw the bikes come in yesterday afternoon; they've got quite a setup, not only at the caravan park but also at the Showground. There were a lot of people in town this morning. The Cyprus Café had a queue out onto the footpath."

"They'll be happy," Joe said.

"Being a coffee addict, which I know you are, when we go into town, I'll take you to the Cyprus Cafe and show you the best coffee in New South Wales." Joe turned to Violet.

Violet's face warmed as she looked back at him with a smile. Not for the first time she thought, what a good-looking man Joe was. Her face got even warmer as his hazel-coloured eyes sparked with interest.

"So, I guess you'll be staying here again tonight because if they're booked out, there's not going to be anywhere else in town to stay. And please, Violet, know that you're most welcome."

Jaclyn turned to Ryan. "I'd invite you to stay at our place, but we have farm sitters arriving the day after tomorrow," Jaclyn said.

"Oh no, I wouldn't put you to any trouble," she said. "It's bad enough that I'm here in Joe's way."

"I'm enjoying the company," Joe said. "Plus, my dishes got washed up, and Violet's one of the few women I've met who appreciates and knows how to make a decent coffee."

"Wow, you have made an impression, Violet," Jaclyn said. "Looks like you better stay here because there's one thing that Joe needs to make him a happy man—his coffee."

Violet smiled at Joe. "If it's not too much trouble, perhaps I could stay here and get you to tow the trailer into town on Monday." She turned to Ryan. "You have no idea how much I appreciate you bringing that car trailer today."

"Monday is fine," Joe said. "I don't have to work all day, because Ryan's closed down for the holidays. Just a small job with Grant in the morning. I could take the trailer in and you could wait until I was finished."

"Have you got accommodation booked ahead with your trip?" Jaclyn asked.

"I don't have to be anywhere until the fourteenth. I've got a job interview down in the Hunter Valley."

"What do you do?" Ryan asked. "If that's not a rude question."

"No, not at all," she said. "I'm an equine vet, and I've got an interview at one of the flash horse studs down near Merriwa. 'Kingdom Horse Stud'."

"Wow, there's some dollars there," Ryan said. "I've passed through a few times; apparently they're owned by one of the Saudi princes, a global thoroughbred giant."

"An equine vet?" Joe asked. "I know that's a horse vet, but what's the difference between that and being a normal vet?"

Violet knew it was time to be honest; this family had been so kind to her. She held Joe's eyes as she explained. "I graduated as a Bachelor of Equine Science after studying for three years at QU. My degree covered equine behaviour, welfare, nutrition, health, reproduction, rehabilitation, exercise, and physiology." It was almost like reading her CV aloud.

Ryan looked at Joe. "Tell Violet how much work there is for her here. No need to go to the big guns in the Hunter Valley."

Joe nodded. "We have a few horse studs around Bindarra Creek who'd jump at the chance of contracting you, Violet. You'd be in great demand, because our horse vet moved away in October. The Smiths up the road, Hannah at Blue Orchard Park, and Lena out on Diggers Road. Did you know Lena bought Anthony Gill's place?" he asked Jaclyn and Ryan.

"I did," Jaclyn said. "Lena's a sweetie. She moved here from California," she explained to Violet.

Violet shook her head. "I didn't know there were horse studs around here when I headed this way. I was heading for t the national park."

Maybe she could spend some time in this area. So far, she'd had a warm welcome and she liked the sound of the town. Plus, if there was some work going it would fill in the time while she waited for her ute to be fixed.

Chapter 10
Violet

Violet rose early on Monday morning as she was keen to get her car sorted and get on her way. Joe's diagnosis, although he had admitted he didn't know much about cars, had worried her, but surely a brand-new vehicle such as hers wouldn't have such a major problem after a few weeks? A glimmer of worry stayed with her, though, as she took a quick shower and walked out to the kitchen.

The coffee pot was on, but there was no sign of Joe. She stood at the window, sipping the coffee that she poured, and smiled as she saw him out past the fence line behind the garage with Molly, walking along beside him. He was altogether way too good-looking, and a nice guy to go with it. Her afternoon yesterday with Joe and his family had filled a need. Her family times and family Christmases were in the distant past now since Wendy had married. Any interactions lately for family occasions at Christmas and Easter had been full of stress: Wendy's husband was a difficult man and didn't like his wife spending time with her family.

Violet had always found an excuse not to accept invitations.

"I have to work." Or, "There's an emergency at the stud." Any excuse she could find.

Wendy knew what it was all about, and Violet was pretty sure that John, her husband, was relieved that he didn't have to put up with the family thing. It hurt, and it was sad, and yesterday, seeing the warmth and love in Joe's family had brought it all home. One day, a few years down the track, she would have something like that. She just needed to get her head together. Forget Brian Bailey, get her car sorted, and fingers crossed, please let this job at the Hunter Valley work out. Working with thoroughbreds was her dream job. There were even a couple of Melbourne Cup winners there. It would be a huge feather in her cap if she could get some experience on those studs.

As she stood there, dreaming, the back door

opened, and Violet jumped, putting her hand to her chest; she hadn't seen Joe walk across the yard. She'd been lost in her thoughts.

"Good morning, Violet, how did you sleep?"

"Very well," she said. "Thank you so much for taking me in and making me so welcome. Yesterday was lovely. I really enjoyed myself. Jac and Ryan are great. And not to forget to mention you and Sam. It was pretty special having a knight on a white charger come down the road and rescue me. I'll never forget it, Joe. I owe you big time."

His eyes were hooded as he regarded her. "You don't owe me anything, Violet. It's been a pleasure to have your company, and you're welcome to stay here, however long it's going to take to get your car sorted."

"Thank you. I might have to take you up on that. Now I just have to worry about my blasted ute, but I really want you to know how much I enjoyed yesterday. And I can't get over Jaclyn offering me her car while they're away."

"It was fun. And yes, I'm very lucky. It was the best decision I ever made to move to town and work with Ryan. Speaking of which, I'm pleased to see you up early because we have to hit the road. I tried to make a couple of calls this morning, but I haven't been able to get onto anyone. The garage isn't open yet, but I do know that Billie Miller is still in town.'

"Is he a mechanic?" Violet asked.

"She is," Luke said. "She's Jonas Miller's daughter. Poor guy has dementia, and I believe she's home for a while to help out. She has her own business in Newcastle and has been helping out casually at Fred's garage.

"I suspect that the problem with your vehicle is the gearbox, but as I said, I'm not a mechanic and maybe it will be just something as simple as an electronic fault or something that's slipped out of place."

Violet chuckled. "I just want to get it fixed and get on the road."

"Are you right to leave about 7:30? I'm working with Grant Cummings today, and I'm only working half a day, so if you're happy to have a wander around town until we get it sorted, we can do that."

"I'll do whatever you say, Joe. We're up two cartons of beer now."

He grinned and didn't comment on that. "I

can show you the coffee shops and a couple of gift shops, and once you see the garage, I should be finished about eleven thirty. We're just doing a small concreting job over Edwina's Fig Tree Lodge. While I'm there I'll get the word out to see if there's anywhere in town for you to stay." He looked at her with a wide smile. "But really, you're quite welcome to stay here. It'll save you some money and to be honest, it's nice to have the company."

"I really appreciate it Joe, but let's not jump ahead and let's see what they have to say about the car."

"What do you want to do with all your gear in the back?"

"That's a good point," she said. "I suppose it's silly to leave it loaded up to go to town, especially if it's going to be there for a couple of days."

"There's room in the small shed. I'll help you unload it before we get going. It'll take a while for us to tow it into town."

"Whoever would've thought I would be been in such a complicated situation when I set off on my trip?"

"You'll be fine. You'll be on the road again

before you know it. And you know what, Violet? When you do move on, I'll miss you. It's been great having company."

She smiled and reached over and put her hand on Joe's, ignoring that tingle that was becoming frequent. "When I say I truly appreciate you having me here. I want you to know I mean it. If it's okay with you, I'll stay on. On one condition: I shop and cook. Deal?"

Joe grinned and squeezed her fingers.

"You've got yourself a deal. Can you bake Anzacs?"

##

Two hours later, Violet was sitting in the Cyprus Café. Joe had driven to town, with her ute on the car trailer behind his car.

Now her the trailer with her ute was parked outside Fred's Garage, which, to Violet's dismay, had been closed when they pulled up. She was pleased that she had taken all of her personal belongings and camping gear out of it because she wouldn't have felt comfortable leaving it parked out the front of an unattended garage. Joe shook his head as they walked across to the office. "Dale usually opens up at six every morning. There must be something wrong," he said with a frown.

Violet clenched her fists at her side, beginning to stress, and Joe noticed straightaway.

"Calm down, Vi. Sorry I mean Violet."

"Vi is fine," she said. "My gran called me Vi."

"Look, I'll take you into the main street and drop you at the café and I'll see what the problem is. Grant'll know what's going on. He's got his finger on the pulse in the town."

"Thank you." Violet pushed back her stress. Joe was on the case and she trusted him.

"I'll give Billie a call, if we can't raise Dale." Joe grinned at her. "And don't say thank you."

Violet followed him to his ute without a word.

"Give me your mobile and I'll call you as soon as I find out."

A couple of minutes later, they turned into Main Street and Joe pulled up at the kerb outside the Cyprus Café.

"Grab a coffee, and tell Nic I sent you. If I

don't call you, it's because I can't find out what's going on. I'll meet you here at eleven-thirty. Have a wander around town." He reached over and took her hand. "And promise me you'll stay calm."

Violet looked at her small white hand enclosed in his tanned and rugged grip, wondering what it was that was sending an array of unfamiliar sensations jangling through her every time Joe touched her.

"You know me well. I promise." She took her hand from his and opened the door, before shooting him a cheeky glance. "And Joe?"

He turned to her with a questioning look.

"Thank you." Violet slammed the door before Joe could reply and she headed for the Cyprus Café.

This was the place that Joe had told her brewed the best coffee he'd ever had. He said the Levonis family had an amazing reputation. "Some people come down here from Tamworth on the weekend just to have lunch here."

Violet entered the coffee shop and looked around with interest. The coffee aroma was certainly enticing as was the array of cakes in the glass cabinet. Even though Joe had said to make herself known to the young guy behind the counter she assumed was Nic, Violet preferred to remain anonymous.

He was a good looking dark-haired young man and his smile was wide as Violet waited at the counter.

'Good morning," he said. "What would you like?"

"I'll—" Her phone dinged in her bag just as she was about to place her order. She ignored it. "A flat white, please. It smells divine."

"Anything to eat? Can I tempt you from our cabinet this morning?"

"It all looks lovely, but no, thank you."

"Where are you sitting?"

"Perhaps a table outside?" she asked.

He took the twenty-dollar note she held out, and rang up her sale and gave her the change. "I'll bring it out shortly."

Violet found a table outside and sat down, pulling out her phone, hoping it was Joe.

No luck: it was a message from her sister

Where are you? Are you alright? I am worried, Violet. Answer me!

Violet quickly sent off a reply. **Sorry, been out of range. All good. Will call later in the**

week. In a national park. I'll let you know where I go to next. Hope all is well, love Violet.

There was no need for Wendy to know she'd broken down, or exactly where she was. Her sister had enough worries without worrying about her. And she was *almost* staying in a national park. Joe's farmhouse was close to it. Wendy would have been horrified to know she was staying with a stranger.

Violet looked up as Nic brought her coffee to the table. On the saucer sat a small pastry roll.

He saw her curious glance and his perfect teeth flashed white in a smile. 'That is our Christmas gift to our customers. A Greek diple, made by my mother."

"It looks delicious," Violet said with a smile. "What is it?"

"It is a traditional Greek sweet, made from dough lightly fried in olive oil and then covered with honey, walnuts and cinnamon."

"Thank you." Nic hurried off as there was a queue forming at the counter and it seemed he was manning the café alone.

Violet finished her coffee and the sweet. She

picked up her bag, slipped her phone inside and decided to explore the town. Joe still hadn't called so she assumed there was no more information about the garage closure. She was becoming desensitised and worrying less every hour. She had a new town to explore, somewhere to stay, and still more than a week to her interview. She would get there, even if it meant catching a bus.

It was still early and many of the shops weren't open yet, so she decided to walk through the town to the garage. She'd taken notice of the route as Joe had driven her to the café. One right turn at Main Street past the grocery store and then follow the Tamworth Road. A brisk walk would do her good.

The distance was further than she'd thought and by the time she got to the garage—which was still closed—Violet was perspiring.

A couple of cars drove in and stopped at the fuel bowsers while she stood there and they then realised the garage was closed and drove out again. An elderly man climbed out of his car, went to the door and peered in as Violet stood in the shade to cool down before she walked back into town.

"Do you know what's going on with the garage?" she asked.

"Yes, it was closed all weekend, because of a family matter," the elderly man replied. "But I did expect Dale to be open today. I hope he opens up soon because I need fuel. I thought he might have put something on the door. I don't like going to the other one."

"Is there another garage in town?" she asked, surprised Joe hadn't mentioned it. "I have an issue with my car and I need a mechanic."

He shook his head slowly. "No, Fred's Garage has the only mechanic in town. He's got a second mechanic working casually too, so you'd think someone could open the place up."

That was the last thing Violet needed to hear. She decided she would have to call the NRMA and see if something could be done.

Today.

Chapter 11
Violet

Violet strolled back to the main shopping street; there were more people around and all the shops were open now. Most of their windows were jazzed up with Christmas decorations. As she turned the corner past the grocery store, she spotted a banner advertising Carols by Candlelight on the sixteenth of December at the local showgrounds.

It was a shame she'd be gone by then—at least she hoped she was—because she'd loved going to the carols with Gran and Pop when she was a child. Violet wandered past the shops, looking into their windows as she filled in time waiting for Joe to finish work; she'd wait until he came to pick her up before she called the NRMA because she wasn't sure where to tell them to come; an whether Joe would suggest leaving the ute on the car trailer in town, or taking it back to the farm.

Violet smiled as she walked along the street,

Christmas carols were coming from a shop ahead. A wave of loneliness hit hard and she wondered where she would spend Christmas Day this year.

Christmas had been a special day back in her childhood days. Gran had always bought her a new Christmas dress, and they'd started the day off with ham and eggs, and after opening the Santa presents, she and Gran would set the Christmas table before the aunts and uncles and cousins had arrived. No matter what the temperature was, a baked dinner followed by hot plum pudding and homemade custard was always served on the long table set up on the high veranda of their Queenslander at West End. Gran had a white damask tablecloth she would iron for hours on Christmas Eve and woe betide anyone who spilled gravy on it.

Violet could almost smell the fresh linen smell as Gran damped it down with a sprinkle from the jug of distilled water. Those days were gone now. Gran and Pop had both passed on when Violet was in her late teens. Then without Gran to keep them in touch, she and Wendy had lost touch with the cousins over the past ten years.

The streets of Bindarra Creek were clean, and the shops neatly kept; it was very different to some of the suburban centres in the city where she shopped at home. It was a pretty street and everyone she passed either smiled or greeted her with a bright "Good morning".

She shook her head as she thought of home. No. It wasn't home anymore; and she wasn't going to have a new home for a long time.

The carols coming from the gallery next to IGA enticed her to enter. The bell tinkled as she pushed the door and walked inside.

"Oh, look at this gorgeous little pot," one of the browsing customers exclaimed. She turned to Violet as she stood by the door looking at the dreamcatchers hanging in the window. "Isn't it pretty?"

"It's certainly unusual," Violet said with a smile. "The colours are gorgeous." The pot was a combination of bronze and pink

The woman behind the counter smiled at them both. "It's one of our local potter's pieces. Jonas—you can see the J on the bottom—was our pastor, but sadly has dementia now, but he's his wife has encouraged him to take up pottery again. He actually was studying art at uni before he realised his calling. His daughter's moved back to town for a few months and is helping out, so we were able to get some of his pieces in for Christmas. They're selling really well. Are you both visiting town?" she asked.

The other customer shook her head. "I'm from Tamworth. I came down with my friend for the day. I'm meeting her back here for coffee after she browses the bookstore. We always do our Christmas shopping in Bindarra Creek. The gift shops here always have something a little bit different. Your gallery and the new gift shop at the Old Butter Factory have some lovely products this year. And when we finish, we always have lunch at the Cyprus Café."

"That's so good to hear. It's good for Bindarra Creek," the woman behind the counter said. "What about you?" She smiled at Violet. "Are you visiting too?"

"Sort of. My car's broken down so I'm spending a few days in town. I'm just waiting for Fred's Garage to open, so the mechanic can take a look at my car."

The woman behind the counter shook her head. "Oh, that's a shame. I heard this morning that Dale won't be back until Friday. Family illness, I think."

Violet's stomach plummeted. Friday!

The woman looked thoughtful. "Has anyone mentioned Billie Miller to you? She's the woman I mentioned who's come back to town to help her mum with Jonas. She's a casual mechanic at the garage."

"Do you have her number?" Violet's hopes rose slightly.

"Better than that. She called me a little while ago. She's on her way down with some more stock for me. I'm Amy, what's your name?"

"Violet Valentine."

"Well, Violet, have a browse for a few minutes. Billie will be here soon."

"Thank you." Violet nodded and crossed to the shelves on the other side of the counter. She would buy some of the goat's milk soap she'd noticed.

The lady from Tamworth took her selection to the counter, and by the time she paid for it and Amy had gift-wrapped her purchases, Violet was waiting beside her with a selection of soaps, and a cute little Paddington Bear door plaque with Georgia on the front. She would give some of the soap to Jaclyn before they left for their holiday. Maybe they could drop it in on the way home today to save Joe bringing her in yet again.

"Morning, Amy."

Violet looked up as the bell over the door tinkled. A woman with shoulder-length blonde hair walked in carrying a box.

"Hi, Billie, Amy said with another smile. "Thanks for bringing some more in. I've nearly sold out of your dad's small pots."

"Well, there's another dozen here if you want them."

"I'll take the lot." Any gestured to Violet. "Billie, this is Violet, she's been waiting to see you."

"Me?" Billie frowned as she looked at Violet with no recognition on her face.

"Hi Billie, you don't know me. I'm a visitor to town. I have some car issues, but the garage is shut, and I didn't call the road breakdown service over the weekend because Joe where I'm staying said they probably wouldn't come until today, so I decided to wait until the garage was open. I thought it might have been quicker, but it looks like I made a wrong call. Amy said you work there?"

"That's right, and yes you would probably have had to wait unless it was an emergency. Usually, Fred's Garage would be your best option, but Dale called me this morning and said to take the week off."

Violet frowned. "I guess it's the NRMA then."

"I'm happy to have a quick look at your car. Where is it?"

"Oh, thank you so much." Finally, some progress. "It's parked at the garage where you work."

"So, it's roadworthy? You can drive it?" Billie asked.

Violet shook her head. "No, Joe Rossiter kindly rescued me when I broke down beside the creek north of his place on Saturday night and his brother lent us a car trailer. It's sitting at the side of the building."

Billie nodded. "How about I take you to the garage now and I can have a look? It might be something simple. If not, you'll have to call the NRMA."

"Oh, would you really? I'll pay you."

"No need. I've got some time on my hands

this morning. What type of car is it?"

"It's a brand-new ute, I've been driving it for six weeks."

"What make?"

When Violet told her, Billie nodded. "I've heard they've recalled their latest model because of gearbox issues. If it is the gearbox, you might be without it for quite a while. Past my expertise."

Violet's spirits sank again. "Well, I suppose I could be stuck in worse places."

"Right to go now?" Billie asked.

"I am. Amy, is it okay if I leave these here? I'll come back when we're done." Violet held up the gifts she'd chosen.

"Of course. Good luck!"

Billie led Violet to a white ute, a much older model than hers, and she gestured to it. "Jump in."

They chatted as they headed down the road.

"Where are you staying in town?" Bille waited at the intersection before the garage.

"Joe's been really kind. I'm bunking in his sleepout. And would you believe his family have even invited me for their early Christmas dinner yesterday.

"They're fairly new to town, but the Rossiters are good people," Billie said. She whistled as she turned into the garage and parked behind the trailer holding Violet's ute. "Brand-new's not wrong!"

Violet nodded glumly. "Yes, brand-new, barely a mark on it, just bit of dust from your dirt roads. There was more dust on it before the rain, and would you believe I broke down in the middle of the creek, about a kilometre from Joe's house. I was heading for the Akuna National Park"

"Can you unlock it and give me the keys?" Billie said. "While I check it out go around the other side of the building and check out the mural. You can see the park there."

"The park?" Violet frowned.

Billie grinned as she took the keys from Violet. "Go and have a stickybeak. It'll make you come back here when you have a vehicle you can rely on." Billie swung herself up onto the trailer, and opened the ute door. The motor turned over but didn't fire, then when Billie tried to put it into gear, there was an awful clunk from underneath.

Violet shook her head and walked towards

the building Billie had pointed out.

A vibrant mural of a river raging through the gorge in the national park with a red-tailed black cockatoo soaring high in the blue arc of sky covered the whole wall.

"Oh wow," Violet murmured to herself. IT must be the national park. She could have camped out there. As she walked back to the ute she thought about the past two nights, and realised she'd enjoyed the time she'd spent at Joe's farm as much—maybe more—as she would have enjoyed camping at the river.

Billie popped the bonnet open and climbed out as Violet walked back to the ute.

"Great mural," she said.

"It is. It's a beautiful spot." Billie looked over the engine and shook her head. "Makes me glad I came back home for a while."

"So, the verdict?" Violet asked?

"Without putting it on the computer, it's hard to say exactly what's wrong, but I'd put money on it being the gearbox. I think you're up for a new one, a gearbox that is; it is the model they've recalled. Sorry to tell you that just before Christmas and while you're on your holiday."

"Oh no, what will I do? There's no point ringing the NRMA, is there?"

"I'd suggest you ring the dealership at Tamworth and inform them that they need to send a truck out here to pick it up, and fix it. The dealership in Sydney I dealt with was difficult to work with, but you might have more luck in Tamworth. The bad news is the gearboxes have to come from China. You'll be pretty lucky to find one in Tamworth, or even in Australia with the number of recalls."

Violet's face fell as she stared at the car. "I guess I made a bad choice."

I'm good at doing that, she thought to herself.

"I didn't look into it enough before I bought it. I just wanted to get a new car fast and get going."

Something else she could blame Brian Bailey for. And then she realised she was being stupid. She should've done more research into buying a car.

"I just expected that something you'd buy this year these days would be reliable." Violet shook her head, thinking of the battle ahead.

"You'd be surprised," Billie said, as they

walked back to her ute after she locked up Violet's car and handed the keys back. "I'll drop you back into town."

"Thank you. Can I shout you a coffee if you won't let me pay you for your time?"

"I'd love a coffee. I was going to head down to the Levonis's cafe after I dropped the pots off. Be good to have company and you can tell me all about how you ended up near Bindarra Creek."

Chapter 12
Violet

Billie leaned back in a chair and pushed her empty cup to the centre of the table. "It's been good having someone to chat to. I hope it all works out for you. Will you stay out at Joe's farm?"

"I think I'll have to. There's no accommodation in town."

"There are a couple of farm stays out on the Tamworth road, but you'd be stuck out there without transport. If Joe's happy to have you there, then stay there," Billie said.

"He's been very kind to me."

"Like I said, a good guy. I met him a few months ago when I first came back to town. You were lucky you broke down where you did."

Violet told Billie the story of Joe rescuing her on the back of a white horse. "The universe was looking after me. For a change."

Billie chuckled. "Sounds like something out

of a romance novel."

Violet shook her head. 'Nope, not for me. That's the last thing I need right now. I'm off men for a long time."

Billie pulled a face. "Tell me about it. Sounds like we need to have dinner together one night, and share war stories."

They swapped phone numbers, and Violet promised to let Billie know how she went with her ute. "If we don't catch up at the pub, I might see you at one of the Christmas events."

Violet nodded. "I saw the Carols by Candlelight banner. Are there other events?"

"There's a Christmas play at the cinema on Saturday night. Sounds like fun, and then the carols the weekend after, and then on Christmas Eve, there's a community picnic with Santa and races and the works. The kids love it."

"Sounds hectic for a sleepy little town."

Billie stood and picked up her cup to take inside to the counter. 'I hope to see you at one of them."

"If Joe comes in, I'll hitch a lift with him, but I don't want to be a nuisance," Violet said. "And thanks for checking out the ute."

Billie gave her a wave as she headed to the

door. "Thank for the coffee. I owe you one."

Violet went to the counter and ordered another coffee. As she was about to pay, she saw Joe's ute drive past. She glanced at her watch; it was just before eleven-thirty; he had mentioned finishing by then. She ordered a second coffee, and paid for them both, and went to wait at the table outside.

"How was your morning?" she asked as he walked up the footpath and sat beside her. A smile lifted her lips. Joe had a smear of paint down the side of his face. "You've been painting.'

"Yep, I finished off the front fence for Mrs Ainslie. It was a short notice job. She's got family coming for Christmas, and wanted the front spruced up. Paddy Cullen, a local bloke who helps out around town was going to do it, but he didn't turn up. How did you know?"

Violet took a serviette off the holder in the middle of the table, leaned over and wiped the side of Joe's face. He hadn't shaved this morning, and there was a sexy dark shadow along his jawline.

"Oh, I guess I have paint on my face too."

"You did," she said.

"Anyway, we got the job done. How was your morning?"

"I picked up a little bit of Christmas shopping. Just a couple of small gifts for Jaclyn and Georgia." Violet patted her bag; she'd collected the parcel from Amy on the way back from the garage. "I discovered the garage is shut until Friday, but I ran into Billie Miller. I've got some good news and bad news."

"Doesn't sound good."

"Billie drove me down to the garage and had a look. That's the good news. The bad news is she thinks it's a gearbox, so your mechanical diagnosis wasn't that far off, and she thinks it will need a new one. Apparently that model has had a recall. It must be in my mail that goes to my sister's now."

Joe scratched his head. "Ouch. So, what's your plan?"

"Billie suggested ringing the dealership in Tamworth and getting it trucked in there to get fixed. She reckons it could be quicker there than the dealer in Brisbane where I bought it."

"Good luck with that," he said. "I'd take you, but it's a little bit far and it's a bit hilly going down that range into Tamworth."

"I wouldn't expect that," Violet said. "I feel so stupid and so useless."

"It's not your fault. A brand-new car that obviously didn't meet standards."

Violet nodded glumly.

"I've got a good suggestion," Joe said. "I'm starving. How about we go around to the pub after we finish our coffee and have a pizza before we go home? I'm done for the day with work."

Violet raised her eyebrows. "Home?"

Joe said, "Okay, home for me, my place for you."

"We really need to sort out what I'm doing. I can't just camp at your place indefinitely."

"Honestly, Violet, I wouldn't expect you to do anything else. Stay. As long as you don't mind being a bit of a way out of town."

"I owe you big time." Her face brightened. "I'll buy lunch."

Joe's grin was wide. "As long as we get two pizzas, I'll accept your kind offer."

Riverside Pub, as the name suggested, was around the corner from the café on the banks of the Akuna River. A delicious aroma came from the kitchen as Joe and Violet walked in.

"Hi Joe," Max, the barman called out, raising his eyebrows with a grin when he saw Violet with Joe.

Joe led her to a table on the back deck of the pub. "It'll be nicer outside," he said. "And there's plenty of shade."

"It's lovely. The river looks beautiful. I saw a mural of it today on the wall of the garage.

"Yes, that's a beauty," Joe said.

Violet looked around as he headed over to the bar to get them a cold drink. Her gaze was drawn to a couple sitting at a table on the other side of the deck. She blinked and then jumped up with an excited cry.

***

Joe chatted to Max as he poured two lemon squash for them. "Few bikes in town," he commented.

"Yeah, you're lucky you came in today. We've been packed every lunchtime since they arrived in town last Friday, but they've got for a ride out to the picnic grounds in the national park today."

"It will only get busier too." Joe handed him a twenty dollar note and waited for the change as Max rang up the sale. "You need any casual staff over the holidays, Max?"

"Sure do. We've been short-staffed every night this week. You interested?"

"I am. I've got my RSA."

"Do you know Dan?" Max asked with a grin.

"The publican? Sure do."

"Okay, I'll have a chat to him and get back to you. Give me your mobile number. How keen are you? Wouldn't mind doing five or six shifts a week? I've been working seven in a row. It'll be great to have the odd night off."

"Happy to take up what's going." Joe wrote his name and number on a coaster and handed it over.

"I'll give you a call later today," Max said.

"Thanks, mate." Joe reached over to pick up the drinks and Max leaned over the bar. 'Who's the looker who came in with you? New in town?"

"A friend. Staying out at my farm for a while." Joe wasn't going to share Violet's business.

"Lucky you."

Joe nodded briefly and picked up the two

drinks and headed outside. Violet's bag was on the floor next to her chair, but there was no sign of her. He looked around and spotted her standing at a table on the other side of the deck. It was Jake and Emma Smith from the horse stud up his road.

Chapter 13

Violet

"Oh, my God, Emma! What are you doing here? I can't believe it. Am I dreaming. And Jake too!"

Emma jumped up and threw her arms around Violet.

"Violet," she squealed. "What are *you* doing here?"

Jake got up with a look of surprise on his around and hugged her. "Last person I expected to see in the pub at Bindarra Creek! Sit down, Violet. Tell us what you're doing here."

"Well," Violet said slowly as she stared into the faces of two of the nicest people she'd ever worked with. "I quit my job and—"

"You what?" Jake said. "I never thought you'd leave Baileys."

"Long story that you really don't want to hear. Things have changed there. But the short story is I'm on the road and my brand-new ute broke down just out of Bindarra Creek." Violet pulled a face. "But tell me, what are you guys doing here?"

"We're having lunch because Mum's here for a few days and offered to mind Nat for us."

"No, I mean here in Bindarra Creek." She wrinkled her nose. "And who's Nat?"

"We live just out of town." Emma beamed. "And Nat is our three-month-old son."

"Hang on. You live here?" Violet asked. "You live here and you have a baby?"

"And we're married." Emma held out her left hand. "We got married in Sydney while Jake was working at Randwick." She looked embarrassed. "It was only a family do, Violet. We didn't invite anyone from Brisbane."

"Don't be silly. Oh wow. I am so out of the loop. I knew you'd moved down to Randwick for a job, Jake. That was the last I heard."

"I did, but it didn't work out. Then Emma's Dad offered to invest in a property we were interested in, and here we are. We've bought our own property, and we're building up our own stud."

Violet's eyes widened. "Tell me about your stud. How far along are you?"

"We've been here two years," Jake said.

Emma's voice was full of pride. 'It's been great, we have two very impressive stallions, thanks to Dad, and they've covered quite a few mares from across the state this season. This spring, our own mares started to foal, and we've got quite a maternity ward going. It's rare for us to be away from the farm like this.'

Finally, Violet realised where their stud was; she'd driven past it on the way in on Saturday.

"Oh my God, you're the Smiths with the stud up the road from Joe! I would never have made the connection with you guys."

"You know Joe Rossiter?" Jake asked.

"I'm staying at his farm. Another long story," Violet said. Her head felt like she was caught in a whirlwind.

"Speak of the devil." Jake stood and shook Joe's hand when he arrived at the table. "Gidday, Joe. Day off?"

Joe nodded. 'Afternoon off, so I thought I'd bring Violet out for lunch. You guys know each other?"

"Know each other" Jake said. "We've known Violet since before she finished uni. When she first started doing work experience, she started doing contract work at the racecourse with Emma's dad."

It looked like Joe was about to get the full history of her working life. At least Jake and Emma didn't know anything about the fiasco with Brian, and Violet certainly wasn't going to mention it.

"Would you like to join us?" Jake asked.

Violet looked up at Joe as he stood beside her chair. "I think you pair were having a day out on your own. You don't want company, do you?"

"Of course, we do!" Emma exclaimed. "We want to hear all about what you're doing in Bindarra Creek and where you met Joe."

Jake nodded. "Grab another chair and sit down, Joe."

"I'll just get my handbag," Violet said.

"Stay there, I'll get it." Joe walked back to their original table and picked up her bag. Violet smiled at him when he handed it to her. "Thank you."

Joe sat between Jake and Violet, and curiosity filled Violet when Emma held her hand up and spoke to her husband. "Jake, are you thinking what I'm thinking?"

"I sure am," he said.

Joe and Violet looked at each other, confused.

Emma leaned forward. "Violet, you said you quit your job?"

'I did."

"Do you have another one?" Jake asked.

Violet shook her head. 'I have an interview Thursday of next week, down at 'Kingdom Stud' in the Hunter Valley."

Emma frowned and looked at Jake.

He shook his head. "A word of warning, Violet."

"And we're not just saying this because we want you," Emma said.

"Want *me*?" Violet's brow wrinkled with confusion. "What do you mean. What for?"

"We've been advertising for someone to work with our horses three days a week. With no luck. There's a shortage of horse vets, as I am sure you know." Emma grinned. "If you took the job, we wouldn't even have to interview you, Vi, because we know exactly how good you are!"

"Hang on, you've advertising for an equine vet?"

"Yes, part-time."

"But what's this warning, Jake?" Violet glanced at Joe. He was following the conversation with interest.

"I've heard that that stud is not a happy workplace there. They go through a lot of staff. There are ads every second week for vets and trainers."

"Okay," Violet said slowly. "So, tell me more about your setup here."

"Where are you staying?" Jake asked.

"I've settled in at Joe's place. As well as rescuing me, he's also very kindly given me his veranda to bunk on."

"Rescuing you?"

Joe chuckled. "I was riding along the creek minding my own business when I encountered a damsel in distress."

"And my rescuer was on a white charger."

Their eyes met and held, and Violet was aware of Emma nudging Jake.

"It's so good to have you here, Violet. Do you think you'll stay?" Emma asked innocently

Violet shrugged. "Depends on my car. I'm making a call after lunch. But I don't plan on settling in the one place yet. I'm going to travel around for a couple of years."

"I never thought you'd leave Baileys," Jake said. 'You almost ran the place."

"Yes, I did, didn't I," Violet said, a hint of cynicism in her voice.

Chapter 14

Violet - three days later

On Thursday, when Violet was driving the small sedan across the creek where her ute had died last weekend, her phone rang. She'd bought another SIM card in town and now had two providers. Today she had the Telstra SIM card in, and that was the number she'd sent to the dealer in Tamworth. It seemed as though a lifetime had passed in the past few days. Joe was working at the farm this morning and she was heading out to the Smiths' stud to have a look around.

Violet had been overwhelmed yesterday; the day Jaclyn and Ryan left to drive to Sydney. She and Joe had been sitting on the back porch, having coffee before he headed out to the paddock for an hour or so. Violet was enjoying the mornings sitting outside chatting to Joe; mist hovered over the paddocks as the early morning sun broke through. She frowned as two vehicles drove in at seven-thirty; she recognised

Jaclyn's red sedan from Sunday lunch, but the Toyota Landcruiser was unfamiliar to her.

"It's Ryan and Jac. Why are they here so early and in two cars?" Joe said. He jumped up and hurried over, and Violet could hear the concern in his voice as she followed close behind him.

"Good morning, guys. Is everything okay? I was going call in and say goodbye when I finished the fence this morning. I was driving Violet to the Smiths' stud in a while and I was going drop over to your place after I dropped her there. Looks like I would have missed you." He peered inside. "Where's Georgia?'

Jaclyn waved to Violet, as she walked around to her open driver's window as Jaclyn stopped the car.

"Hi Jaclyn, good to see you again."

"This will help you with the shopping." Jaclyn held out her car keys as she climbed out of the car.

"The shopping?" Violet frowned. "Help me?"

"We know that you're having car problems and you might be in town for a little while, so we thought it was silly to have my car sitting at home while we're away. So, we brought it out for you to use, Violet."

Violet's mouth dropped open, and she shook her head. "Oh, that's so kind of you, but there's no need to."

"Yes, there is. If you're staying here for a while, you certainly don't want to be stranded while Joe is busy. I'd love you to use it."

Violet's eyes pricked with tears. She wasn't used to such kindness. She walked over to Jaclyn and hugged her. "Well, then I accept, and thank you very much. I'll look after it well. I've told Joe if he won't take any rent from me while I'm waiting for my car to be fixed, the least I can do is shop and cook. And it will get me over to Jake and Emma's if I accept their offer."

"Their offer?"

"They've offered me some work while I'm here." She didn't mention when she and Emma had gone to the ladies' room on their way out on Monday, that Emma had offered her a full-time permanent contract.

"Not permanent, Em. I'm not ready yet," she'd said.

"Something bad happened in Brisbane,

didn't it?" Emma asked. "I can see it in your eyes. You're not the bubbly Violet of old."

"I'm an older and wiser Violet these days. I'll tell you about it later. When I come out to see your place."

She hadn't mentioned the hint of permanent work to Joe.

"That's great news," Jaclyn said. "All sorted then. Come on, Ryan. We're on a deadline."

Ryan rolled his eyes. "The story of my life, Violet. Jac runs our household like she runs her school."

"And that's why we're organised ready to go." Jaclyn grinned. "We've got the suitcases packed at home. Cleo is sitting with Georgia while we do a last few things in town, and we'll leave when she'd due for her afternoon nap."

"Hang on for a minute." Violet hurried inside and brought out the two small gifts. She was extra pleased now she'd made the effort.

'Thank you, you shouldn't have." Jaclyn gave her a quick hug. "I hope you're still here when we get home, Violet."

"No word on your ute yet?" Ryan asked as Jaclyn walked around to get into the Landcruiser.

"Just that it needs a new gearbox. I'm supposed to hear today, but I won't hold my breath." The company had been difficult to deal with when Violet had called after lunch on Monday. "So, fingers crossed."

They waved Ryan and Jaclyn off, and Joe went inside to put his work boots on while Violet went inside for her bag. "I'll go and see Emma and Ryan now. I'll be back to get your lunch." She frowned. "Should I take Jaclyn's car through the creek?"

"Not a problem. Their creek is much deeper than mine, Anyway I looked there yesterday afternoon. Since the rain's gone, there's only a few centimetres running across the causeway now. And don't rush home. I can make myself a sanger," he said. His grin sent the usual tingles of warmth through her. She was getting altogether too comfortable at Joe's place. If she was still in town after Christmas when the accommodation in town freed up a bit, she'd move out. A bit of distance might stop the attraction that was building.

You do not need a man in your life, she told herself sternly.

Joe gave her a wave as he headed to the

shed, and Violet opened the door of Jaclyn's car.

"Give me a buzz on the landline if you hear from the dealership, won't you?" he called out.

"I will, but if it's bad news, I'm not going to be in a very good mood."

"How about we go out to the pub for tea tonight? You've cooked the last two nights, and it's been wonderful. I think we need to give you a break."

"I enjoy cooking, but I will have to go shopping in town this afternoon."

"If we go out you can leave it until tomorrow. We'll go into the pub. Last chance, almost, because I'll be working there from Friday night."

"Okay, sounds good."

Now Violet turned to her phone as it rang; it was the dealership in Brisbane.

"Violet Valentine speaking."

"Good morning, Mrs. Valentine," the gruff voice said. "It's John Bainbridge from the All Autos dealership on Ipswich Road."

"Good morning, Mr. Bainbridge. I hope you've got some good news for me."

"Well, sort of. Good and bad, love," he said.

"I need to ask you about where you've been driving the vehicle to see if it's covered under warranty. And what you've been towing."

Violet's temper fired. She'd had enough of being treated badly in Brisbane and wasn't about to take bullying from the car dealer.

"It will be covered under warranty because I only purchased the car from you six weeks ago. It's done less than 2000 km and it has never towed anything."

"But where did you take it? There's a bit of red dirt on the wheels, and our dealership at Tamworth told me there's a broken arm on the gearbox. Have you been travelling on dirt roads?"

"I have, and that certainly does not preclude the warranty being implemented. The vehicle has never been in four-wheel drive. Yes, it has been on the odd gravel road, and I forded one creek, but I certainly haven't done anything to break an arm on a gearbox. It's obviously poor workmanship or shoddy components."

"Okay, I'll admit we've had a few problems with this model," he said. "I think some of the Chinese steel isn't the quality we're used to."

"Well, John. That's not my problem. I'm

sorry I ever bought it off you," Violet said. "I would prefer a refund."

His laughed boomed over the phone and the sound reminded Violet of Brian Bailey. She shivered.

"Well, no need for that. It'll be repaired, love. Good as new."

"It is new!" Violet exclaimed.

'Well, you'll have your lovely new ute back in eight weeks or so."

"What! No way. I can't go eight weeks without my car. I have commitments."

"We've got some courtesy cars at the dealership on Ipswich Road. We are quite happy for you to collect one and drive around Brisbane in it."

"I'm seven hundred kilometres away from Brisbane at the moment, and I'm stranded on a farm. Without the brand-new vehicle. I remind you I paid sixty thousand dollars for that vehicle in good faith."

"Well, love, I can't do anything for you. They're shipping your vehicle from Tamworth up to Brisbane. I wondered why you took it to your Tamworth dealership and why you didn't bring it to us."

Duh, because it was broken down.

Violet rolled her eyes. It sounded as though the guy wasn't the brightest tool on the shelf, but then to be fair he was in the sales and warranty area and didn't know much about the mechanical side of things.

"Because it broke down in the country near Tamworth." She kept her voice patient, despite wanting to yell at him.

"Rightio."

"Who should I call if I want an update on the 'or so' you said?"

"Just call my number. You've got it in your phone now, love."

"I have" Violet cringed at the 'love'.

"You have a wonderful day," he said and disconnected.

Violet shook her head and headed for the Smiths' place. Excitement fizzed when she turned up the long drive and saw a beautiful black stallion grazing in the front paddock.

She was beginning to enjoy this country life.

Chapter 15

Joe

Joe put the peanut butter back in the fridge and smiled as he noticed how tidy the shelves were. Picking up his coffee in one hand and the plate with his sandwich in the other, he wandered out to the back porch. He loved sitting out there, looking out over the paddocks and his sheep run where his girls were happily grazing. It always soothed him, and he needed soothing now.

When people talked about love at first sight, he used to grin and say that only happened in the movies.

He'd been wrong.

Joe had known the instant he'd spotted Violet spotted in her campsite at his creek that his life was about to change.

He'd fallen instantly and hard. It wasn't just that she was such an attractive woman; it was her goodness and kindness, her patience and interest in other people. Her willingness to listen as he talked to her about his sheep at dinner every night.

He was head over heels already, but he hadn't done anything about it, and he told himself he wasn't going to. He wasn't good enough for Violet Valentine. She'd been to university, and from all accounts listening to Jake and Emma at the pub the other day, she was a well-respected equine vet, and the fact that they wanted to employ her as soon as they knew she was in town supported that.

I didn't even finish high school, so how on earth could I even consider having a relationship with someone with Violet's smarts, motivation, and a solid career behind her?

Joe had spent his first eight years out of school as a shearer, travelling the country and having a good time, learning about sheep, and the land. Saving to buy his own place, and he was damn proud that he had. But his modest little farm wasn't enough for a woman of Violet's calibre.

Now, at least, he had two steady jobs with Grant and Ryan, and even though he learned a lot and was a good chippie and landscaper, he still hadn't been to TAFE and was pretty much just a labourer.

He made a pact with himself as he stared out over his land.

He would enjoy Violet's company for as long as she stayed, and he would help her as much as he could. He would avoid the finger brushing, the touching on the shoulder, and the lingering eye gazing; it wasn't doing him the slightest bit of good. Being out of the house working at the pub at night would help too, and if she was out during the day, maybe he could get over this hopeless infatuation. Then when she moved on, he would look for a suitable woman.

***

Violet parked outside the house paddock at Jake and Emma's. The lush front lawn was edged with colourful spring flowers; six bottlebrush trees loaded with pendulous crimson spikes ran along the fence near the front gate. The red and green combination made it look like Christmas in the garden.

Taking a big, deep breath of country air and listening to the birdsong in the trees as she looked out over the lush pastures, calm gradually stole over Violet. There was nothing she could do. She would be eight weeks without her ute, and once it was fixed, she'd think about trading it in and getting something else. She wasn't going to risk that happening again as she travelled around the country.

And there was nothing she could do with her attraction to Joe. She'd just ride it out and let events take their course. Sitting at the dinner table last night, eating the meal she'd cooked had been very homely, and she relaxed even more in his company. After dinner, Joe had insisted on washing up; his dishwasher still hadn't arrived. Violet went into the living room, sat on the comfortable sofa, and chose a book from Joe's collection; they had the same taste in authors. Half an hour later, after he had been out and fed Molly, he came into the living room, turned the television on, and sat on the sofa beside her. They watched the seven o'clock news together.

Violet had started to giggle halfway through the program.

Joe turned to her with a grin. "What?"

"All I need is some knitting and we'd make the perfect domestic scene."

As soon as Vilet spoke, she regretted

voicing her thoughts, but Joe had laughed and held her gaze thoughtfully

They were very much at ease in each other's company, and she was thoroughly relishing the freedom and the lack of stress.

And looking at Joe. But she wouldn't go there. Whatever happened she would deal with.

She pulled her thoughts back to the present as Emma ran lightly down the front steps.

"Well, that looks much more like the Violet of old," she said as Violet gave her a happy smile. "Coffee's on, Nat's asleep and Jake's up at the stables. Now come and tell me why you really left Brisbane."

An hour later, Violet had spilled the whole story to Emma, who shook her head in disbelief as Violet described how the emotional bullying from her boss—who had slowly then become her boyfriend—had escalated.

"I can't belief that you were going out with Brian," Emma said as she poured their second cup of coffee. "He was always a sleaze."

"I know," Violet said. "And I'm ashamed that I did get into a relationship with him. He bullied me into it. The clever comments, the constant negativity, and the gradual erosion of my self-worth. I was actually grateful to him when he asked me out for dinner the first time."

"Ugh." Emma shuddered.

"At least I didn't move in with him, but when I wouldn't, he half-moved into my apartment. No matter how much I tried to get him to go home after we'd been out, he'd insist on staying. And then his toothbrush appeared next to mine, and his shaving gear went in my cupboard."

"Total control," Emma said, reaching over to squeeze Violet's hand.

"I took great pleasure in putting all of his stuff in the bin when I left." A giggle escaped her. "It was one of those eight-hundred-dollar Braun shavers."

"You go, girl! See the old Emma was still in here."

"Yes, but when I was with him, I couldn't see that what he was doing was so toxic, and it took an incident at the stables to really wake me up. We lost a horse, and Brian told everyone that it was my misdiagnosis and subsequent treatment that had caused the problem. I hadn't even been near the poor creature. He had, and he put the blame on me. I was so angry my common sense came roaring back and I realised what I'd let him do to me."

"No, you realised what he had done to you. No 'letting' about it. So, you told him to pee off?"

Violet shook her head and stared out the window over the beautiful rolling paddocks.

"No, I was too scared of him. He went to a conference in Sydney for a week, and then toured some studs in the Southern Highlands for the second week. He tried to make me go, but I could see my chance and refused. I bought the ute in a rush—foolishly as it has turned out—and I took off. Even Wendy, my sister doesn't know where I am." She widened her eyes. "Please don't tell anyone in Brisbane. I know he'd come after me."

"We don't know anyone up there now. Most of our equine friends are in Sydney and the Hunter Valley. That's how Jake knew so much about that stud you applied to. Are you still going for that interview?"

"No. I wasn't thinking straight. I realised I couldn't take any references, so it would be a waste of time. If I had, it would get back to

Brian."

"Oh, Violet. You poor thing. But there's always a silver lining. First, you ended up here where's there's plenty of work, and you don't need references. If you don't want to commit to us, just take it week by week. We'd be happy to have you for as long as you want to stay. Stay here and get your confidence back. Plus, there's a few other studs around the district."

"And what was second"? Violet asked.

Emma's smile was crafty. "Joe."

"Joe?"

The chemistry between you both virtually crackled in the air at the pub the other day. I saw the way he was looking at you the whole time. And I know that you're not immune to him."

"How on earth did you see that." Violet's cheeks burned and she dropped her face into her hands. "Have I made a total fool of myself?"

'No, you just looked like two people really happy to be in each other's company."

Violet lifted her head slowly. "I am. He's the kindest and most considerate person I have ever met."

"Not to mention, a bit of a honey to look at."

Emma chuckled. "Just go with the flow, and let things take their course, sweetie."

"Wise advice."

"We're going to the Carols by Candlelight at the showground next Saturday," Emma said "Why don't we all go together?"

"Sounds good. Even if Joe's working at the pub, I'll come."

"No. that's not what I meant. I'll get Jake to ring him and tell him to see if he can have the night off."

"Emma, you haven't changed a bit!"

Her long-time friend jumped up; her face alight with love. "Here comes Jake now. Come and we'll show you around, and tempt you to stay."

Chapter 16
Violet

On the drive into the Riverside Pub for dinner late that afternoon, Violet talked nonstop about the Smiths' horse stud.

"Their stables are state of the art, their horses are superb, and best of, they are the best couple anyone could ever ask to work with."

Joe glanced at her as he changed back a gear. "So, sounds like you're going to take the job."

"Only on a month-to-month basis. I'll see what happens with the ute."

"So, the dealer still haven't rung?" Violet put her hand over her month. "Woops, I forgot to tell you."

"Good news then?"

"I guess it depends which way you look at it."

"What do you mean?" Joe frowned.

'Eight weeks at least. They've trucked it back to Brisbane to wait for a gearbox."

She glanced across at Joe and caught the glimmer of a smile on his lips.

'What about the job in the Hunter Valley?" he asked.

"I've decided to pass on that."

Violet smiled as a big grin spread on Joe's face. "That is good news."

"Because you don't have to drive me down there now?" she teased.

"No." He shot her a warm glance. "Because you'll be staying for a while."

The pub was buzzing. Joe greeted every second person as they made their way through the crowd in the bar between the entry and the bistro. He reached back and took her hand so she could keep up with him, and Violet didn't let go.

What did Emma say? Go with the flow.

Joe had rung and reserved a table and they were out on the corner overlooking the river again. A patch of mown lawn ran between the veranda and the water; half a dozen children were playing tag on the grass.

"What would you like to drink?" he asked as he held her chair out for her.

A gentleman. No one had ever done that for

Violet before.

"Will we have pizza?" she asked.

"I will, but you don't have to, if you don't want it. '

"I do. It smells great. So, if we're having pizza, I'll have a red wine."

"What sort of pizza do you like? I'll order when I get our drinks."

"Surprise me. I love it all." Happiness surged through Violet as Joe smiled at her and turned to the bar. The atmosphere, the aromatic garlic fragrance permeating the room, the thought of a red wine, and most of all Joe's company in a town she was beginning to love.

He paused and turned back to her.

"Promise me one thing?"

Violet tipped her head to the side. "Promise what?"

"Christmas last year, I brought a newcomer to town to the pub for pizza. Turned out Leah was here to get over a broken heart, but when I got back from ordering, she'd spotted her lost love across the room. I had to eat the whole pizza by myself."

"And were you heartbroken?" Violet asked.

"No, Leah and Mark are married now. They

went back to Sydney. I went to their wedding in June, and I was pleased to see how happy they were."

Violet sat back as Joe headed across to the bar. He was well liked, he chatted as he made his way across; he was patient and had a smile for everyone. Her heart did another little flip in her chest and she pulled herself up. She was overreacting to a nice guy, and it was only because of the bad experience she'd had with Brian.

Nothing more. There was no need to go with the flow like Emma said.

"Penny for your thoughts? Did you decide you don't want pizza after all?" Joe put two glasses of ruby-red wine on the table and sat down. He pulled the buzzer from his shirt pocket and put it in the centre of the table. "You look worried. Our mum used to say a problem shared is a problem halved; this is more than your car worrying you, isn't it?"

She leaned back, put her hands on the table, and stared back at him. "Do you have ESP, Joe Rossiter?" she asked with a smile; his green eyes were mischievous as he held her gaze.

"No, I just like to know what's wrong. You

looked very worried when I turned around and walked across with our drinks.

"Joe, you don't have to worry about me."

"It's what friends are for," Joe said. "And I think we've already established a friendship, haven't we, Violet?"

"We have, and I'm enjoying getting to know you better. I was just thinking about work." It was a little white lie; she didn't want to say she'd been thinking about him."

"You were so animated on the way into town, about their stud." Joe reached over and put his hand on hers. "And Vi? I'm really enjoying getting to know you too, and I have no worries at all about you staying. As long as it takes to get your car fixed, you're welcome to stay, but you already know that. I'd like to get to know you even better. Now, tell Uncle Joe what's really on your mind." He saw straight through her.

"Well, I won't tell you the whole story, but I've left Brisbane for good, and I'm really unsure of where I want to end up."

"Tell me more about your job. You're a vet, but I guess an equine vet is horses only? Tell me *exactly* what you do."

As Violet described her job to him, Joe's hands stayed on hers, and the warmth of his skin sent a tingle up her arm. She had never met such a good listener; her friends from work that she had gone out with after Emma and Jake had left, in the before-Brian days, had all been pretty superficial. That's why she had been sucked in so much by Brian. He'd filled a need for friendship to begin with

"So why did you leave your job in Brisbane? Had enough of it?"

Violet bit her lip and dropped her gaze, and his hand tightened on hers slightly. She was dismayed when she lifted her head and felt the tears prick her eyes.

"I'm sorry I didn't mean to upset you. Was it something bad?"

"It was actually. I let myself get bullied. I thought I'd fallen for this guy, my boss, of course, but he was just an absolute manipulator, and over the course of about six months, he really made me lose my confidence. Just little things. I mean, there was no physical bullying or anything like that, and he was as nice as pie to me when we were out. But when we were in the workplace, he always questioned my decisions, always had something negative to say. When I asked for his opinion, he always criticised me. And it took me a good six months and the death of a horse for me to realise it was a really unhealthy relationship. Work and otherwise. So, I left. It's left me a bit sad, but I feel safe here"

No need to mention, she was absolutely scared Brian would come looking for.

"Safe is a strange word to use. It wasn't a good job if you were bullied. I'm sure there's a big call for equine vets around the country. I mean, how many horses are there?"

"Lots," she said with a smile. She lifted her hand from his and put hers on top of his and squeezed his fingers. "You're a good listener, Joe."

"That's me," he said. "Not a lot more that I'm good at."

"Rubbish, you have two jobs, you have a brilliant farm under development and I think you're a man of mystery as well," she said with a wide grin. Before he could reply, the buzzer buzzed on the table, and Joe jumped up. "I'll get our tea."

He came back with two plates and cutlery

in one hand and a huge rectangular tray of pizza in the other. The enticing aroma of garlic and cheese tickled Violet's nose, and her mouth watered.

"Oh, yum, that smells wonderful."

"Best pizza anywhere."

"Not a bad town by the sound of things. Best pizza, best coffee, great Christmas shopping, friendly people." She pulled a face. "But no garage, no fuel."

"There's a fuel pump at the station on the other side of town. There's just no mechanic there. There's a bit of a restaurant and a fuel stop, so you can get fuel."

"Yes, I knew that, I was just teasing. I could get fuel if I had a car that was going," she chuckled.

Joe reached out and took her hand again. "It's so good to see you smile. Now hoe in, before I eat it all."

***

Joe

When the tray was clear of pizza, Violet grabbed his hand and insisted they finish their wine at the railing overlooking the river. She leaned back on the timber and put one hand to her stomach.

"Oh, my goodness, I don't think I'll eat again this week," she said. "That was divine."

The sun was setting in a blaze of glory, and the soft breeze lifted strands of her blonde hair as Joe stood close to her. The laughter of children playing drifted up from the lawn, and the first twang of a guitar chord announced the night's music was about to begin.

Violet's hair glowed gold in the late afternoon sunlight, and Joe's eyes travelled down from her dark brown eyes. She obviously worked out. Her knee-length floral dress hugged her figure, and the muscles in her legs and her arms were well-defined. He guessed you'd have to be pretty fit if you're working with animals the size of horses.

Violet picked up her wine and the last of ray of sunlight glinted on her glass as she raised it to her lips. Half the blood in Joe's body travelled south, and he gripped his wine glass and cleared his throat.

"Would you like another one?" he managed to choke out.

"No, thanks. I know you can't have another one and drive, so let's home. I think there are a few people waiting for a table. I'd like to get back early. I was a bit worried about Molly tonight. I think she's fairly close to having her pups."

"I thought that too. Come on, madame, your chariot awaits."

It was natural to put to put his arm around Violet's waist to steer her through the crowd. and out to the car park. It felt right.

Violet shook her head after half the bar said goodnight as they walked through "What is it with this town? Do you all take nice pills or something?"

Her eyes held his intently. "It's just nice to be able to help somebody in need. That's what friends are for, Vi."

Chapter 17
Violet

Violet woke up on Saturday with a smile on her face. If anyone had told her last Saturday when she broke down that within a week her car would be on the way to Brisbane to get a new gearbox installed, she would be staying in a farmhouse at Bindarra Creek with one of the loveliest guys she had ever met, and had started working in her chosen field at Jake and Emma's place, she wouldn't have believed it. She shook her head as she stepped out of the kitchen. She'd heard Joe up earlier and smiled when she noticed the cup left out for her next to the coffee machine. He must be out in the paddock because his ute was still out there

Joe was going into town this morning. Apparently, Grant Cummings, whom she hadn't met yet, had left him a small job to do by himself today as he and his partner, Cathy had gone to the coast for a pre-Christmas holiday. Violet poured her coffee and went out to the back step, looking out over Joe's paddocks. The rain from last weekend's storm had turned the grass an emerald-green, and the sheep grazed happily in the paddock where Joe was in the process of replacing the fence.

All that was needed to make it a perfect picture, she thought, was a couple of chestnut horses – her favourite colour. She shook her head as she wandered over to the fence; that wasn't going to happen. This was Joe's place, and she was only here temporarily.

She didn't want to settle yet, but it was hard to think of moving on because she had never experienced an attraction like the one that was building.

Joe had been so kind to her ever since he'd charged in on his dashing white horse. As Violet wandered along the fence; Sam came over and nuzzled into her.

"Good morning, you rogue, and I'm sorry, there's nothing in my pocket."

She walked to the end of the fence and stood there, looking at his sheep. It was such a clear day she could see the top of the hills over the Akuna National Park, and she promised herself she would get there to camp one day.

But today, while Joe was working, she intended to go to IGA and do a good grocery shop. It was the least she could do with him letting her stay here. He wouldn't even consider any rent, so she was going to fill the cake tins this afternoon.

And bake a double batch of Anzacs.

***

Joe

Joe gripped the steering wheel tightly as he headed into town to do a small concreting job for Grant. The concrete mixer was still on-site where Joe needed it, but he had to call into the rural store on the way and pick up a bag of concrete. It was another small concrete pad for Mrs Ainslie; she had so many pots in her garden she was gradually getting her whole lawn concreted.

Joe sighed as he turned onto the road to town. He was caught between a rock and a hard place. He'd been a bloody fool. An idiot who couldn't keep his mouth shut. He'd made a total idiot of himself.

This morning after he'd come in from the paddock, Joe chuckled when Violet announced her intention to clean out the linen cupboard where she'd found the old linen she'd used for setting on the tale at their Christmas dinner last weekend. Molly mooched around their feet, still heavy with her pups. "I'll do a shelf every morning before I go to the stud."

"Don't worry about it," he said. "It's only old stuff."

"Old stuff!" Violet shook her head and grabbed his arm "Joe, you've got no idea what's in there. You can't just sit there and let it rot. I'll go through it for you and I'll sort it into things you might like to give some to Jaclyn. And maybe put some aside for Georgia for when she grows up, plus there's plenty there that you can use now."

A strange look crossed her face as he stared back at her—as though she wasn't interested in what he thought.

Joe quickly dropped his gaze. "Fine, we'll use it until you move on, and then I'll be sitting at the kitchen table eating by myself."

"Don't be silly. Look at that big Christmas dinner you organised for Jac and Ryan. I'm sure you'll do that again and get use out of it. Anyway, I feel like a clean out. But if you'd prefer I don't touch your stuff, you just have to say."

It was the first time he'd seen her cross.

"That dinner was a one-off; we only had it here because they were going away. We have Christmas at their farm every year."

"Joe," she said sensibly, and he hated her tone. "One day I'm sure you'll meet somebody, and you will have a wife—or a partner, I don't know whether you believe in weddings or not— I'm sure you'll have a tribe of kids too. This farm just cries out for a family to live and love in it. If I ever come back this way in a few years, I'll drive past, and when I see a swing set and a trampoline outside the house, I'll know I was right."

Joe lifted his eyes again, and he held hers steadily. "The problem is I can't have the person I'd like to marry because she's too good for me," he said.

"I didn't know you had a girlfriend, Joe. I didn't know there was someone on the scene. I hope she doesn't mind me being here. And how can you not be good enough? You are a fine man."

He'd taken a step closer to her as they stood

in the narrow hall, near the cupboard.

He reached out and took her hand. "I'm sorry, Violet. I wasn't going to say anything, but I can't help myself. I know I'll sound stupid. It's only been a week since I found you stranded down near my creek, and Sam and I rescued you."

"Don't forget Molly too," she said with a smile, still not getting what he was trying to say.

Tension flared along all his nerve endings as Violet looked up at him, but it was still a pleasant sensation feeling her hand in his. He didn't take his eyes off her.

"You don't get it, do you?" he said, shaking his head. "I don't think you'd even consider me."

"Me?" she said, frowning. "Consider you for what? What are you talking about, Joe?"

"I never believed all those romance stories, when you can fall for a woman in an instant. But Vi, I fell hard from that first moment I saw you standing there when I rode along on Sam. I've got to know you over the past week, and my feelings just kept getting stronger. I never believed in love at first sight, but I guess it happens."

Her cheeks went bright red as she stared at him, her mouth opening.

"You've . . . you've overwhelmed me, Joe. I don't know what to say." Her eyes filled with tears. "I'm really flattered, but I can't stay. I'm not ready to settle anywhere."

"I'll be late home tonight," he said gruffly as his hope sizzled into ashes. 'I'm working at the pub. I'll see you tomorrow."

He'd turned away, grabbed his keys and got in the ute.

Chapter 18
Violet

Violet felt so bad about Joe spilling his heart to her, she needed to talk to someone. She finally messaged Wendy to tell her where she was and that she had decided to stay in Bundarra Creek for a few weeks. She still hadn't told her about her broken-down car, so she didn't get an "I told you so." Wendy had called her straight back and it was really good to hear her sister's voice. It helped her take her mind off Joe; she just didn't want to think about that.

She couldn't stay. She wasn't ready. It was too soon.

If she told herself often enough, maybe she'd believe it.

"Where are you staying?" Wendy went straight to the point. 'There's some mail here for you. I need to send it on."

"On a farm about fifteen kilometres out of town. Post it; I'll be here for a while, I think.

You'd love it here. Why don't you come down for a visit?" It was a strategic move on Violet's part; she knew that would stop any more questions from her sister.

But she was surprised by her answer. "I will. how long are you staying there?"

"I'm not sure yet. I'm doing a little bit of work at a local horse stud, so who knows what will happen." She was as vague as she could be.

"Well, if you're still therein the New Year, I will come down and visit."

Violet pulled out a chair and sat down on Joe's back porch. "So, you'd really come and visit me?"

"Yes, there have been a few changes at home," Wendy said slowly.

"What sort of changes?"

"Not exactly changes. It's a bit of a quantum shift," Wendy said enigmatically.

"Tell me, sis."

"Jerry's moved out. But I guess it was always going to happen."

'Are you all right?"

The tone in her sister's voice reassured her. "Actually, I've never been better. We should have done it a long time ago. We're actually talking civilly now How are you?"

"I'm okay. Actually, I'm good. I'm happier than I've been for a long time."

"I'm pleased you left. I knew what was going on, but you had to realise for yourself, Violet."

"It took me a while."

"He's looking for you, sis. That's another reason I rang. Just be careful."

"Brian came to your place?"

Violet gasped. "You didn't tell him, did you?"

Wendy laughed but there was no mirth in it "How could I tell him when I didn't know until now where you are? I still don't have a clue where you are because I've never heard of Bundarra."

"Bindarra Creek. It's a magical town," Violet said softly.

"Magic or not, just take care."

Violet headed off to the stud once She ended the call with Wendy, and was surprised to find a note on the front door from Emma.

Sorry, tried to call. We've gone to the Tamworth. Jake said could you please have a look at Lady Duo's teeth, he thinks there's a

problem. Not eating well and bad breath. We'll be home late so don't hang around.

Every time Violet passed a car on the way home—and for some reason there seemed to be more today, or perhaps she was just more aware, she looked for Brian.

She turned into the Joe's driveway around four o'clock that afternoon, and stared as she noticed a vehicle near the shed. Her heart started beating hard, and then she realised it was Joe's; he mustn't have had to work the shift at the pub.

It wasn't Brian. She had to get out of that mindset; there was no way he would know where to find her.

Tired and dirty—dealing with an abscess and injecting antibiotics had been a messy business, Violet yawned as she parked Jaclyn's car next to Joe's ute.

She sat on the back steps, took her filthy boots off, and washed her hands at the concrete trough beside the old toilet adjacent to the back door. There was no sign of Joe, so she guessed he was avoiding her after his bombshell this morning. She knew he'd been trying to get the fence finished off in the girls' paddock. He'd told her about the interesting enterprise he was starting. He had been full of anticipation and excitement when he described it to her, talking about growing wool for the home spinners and his plans to market it.

Violet had helped him a couple of afternoons ago; it had been great fun out there in the heat, chasing the flies away and laughing while working together. She hadn't done much; she'd pretty much just passed tools as he'd asked for them, but Joe said it was good having her company out there.

After a quick shower, Violet brewed a pot of coffee, poured a cup, and browsed the internet on her phone. There were a few more jobs up, including a local ad for an equine vet at a stud called Blue Orchard in Bindarra Creek. She took a screen shot; it didn't hurt to cover all bases.

Joe had been so pleased when she'd decided to stay local, but he'd obviously missed the point it was only a short-term stay.

"It already feels like you've been here for ages. Very handy having you around the house," his green eyes were mischievous, "and I'm eating much better than I usually do too," he'd said.

"Well, I'll have to teach you how to cook in the next few weeks."

After this morning, she guessed he was going to avoid her. It was time to look for somewhere ese to stay, but if she was honest, Violet knew she wanted to stay here.

With Joe.

An hour and a half later, she checked the time on her phone as concern began to trickle through her. It was very late for him to be out working; the sun had been down for almost an hour, and it was almost too dark to see the house paddock now.

Normally, he would check the fences in the afternoon, feed the animals, and come back in. They'd sat on the back porch every afternoon, having a sundowner as they watched the sunset together and talked.

Maybe he was working late because he hadn't wanted to do that. They had to nut this situation out, or she had to leave. It wasn't fair if he was staying away from his own home because she was there. But how did you discuss something like that?

Violet looked at the time again and decided

to go check if he was okay. She put on a pair of boots and socks, always aware of the snake danger at this time of the year. Heading out to the stables and the dog pen, she noticed Sam grazing in the small paddock behind the stables, but the gate to the dog pen was open, and there was no sign of Molly.

She knew where Joe went every afternoon because two nights ago, she'd walked out with him. Violet hadn't realised that the creek actually turned this way and wound through his property. There was a lovely little glade at the back of the paddock he'd fenced off for his sheep.

She whistled for Molly as she walked toward the sheep paddock behind a stand of gum trees. Cocking her head, she heard a distant bark coming from the direction of the creek. Well, if Molly was over there, she must be with Joe. When she walked another hundred metres, she started to call him.

"Joe, are you there?" Luckily, she'd thought to grab a torch because it was now pitch dark. There was no moon. She switched the flashlight on, directing it on the ground ahead of her.

"Joe, are you out here?"

Another bark.

Violet picked up her pace, hurrying along the fence line until she reached the intersection where the sheep paddock started. Molly's barking was getting closer, and she listened.

"Joe, can you hear me?"

"Violet? I'm over here." His voice was faint.

"Where is here?" she said.

"At the end of the fence near the creek," he called. Molly kept barking, obviously recognising Violet's voice.

Violet set off on a light run, watching where she was stepping with the light shining on the ground ahead of her. She stopped and flashed it around the trees, seeing the end of the fence only about thirty metres away.

"Where are you, Joe? I can't see you."

"A bit further ahead of where you are."

"Where?" she called back.

"Keep coming! I can see your torch. Just keep straight ahead, and then when I yell out, veer a little bit to the right."

Violet wasn't game to ask if he was okay. He obviously wasn't. She couldn't see him so he must be on the ground.

It was only a minute or so later when he called again and his voice was louder. "Good, come into the bush now, I'm just in here." She ran over and Moly gave a strange bark and then flopped to the ground, whimpering beside Joe.

Violet tried not to panic as she shone the light on both of them. Joe's face was pale and he was perspiring heavily.

'What's wrong? What have you done. It's not a snake bite, is it?"

"No, I've wrenched my shoulder, and I think Molly's about to have her pups too," he said.

"What on earth did you do?" she asked, crouching beside him.

"Stupid, actually. I was walking along here, checking out a place to dig for the new posts, and I obviously came across an old hole. My foot went into it. I didn't hurt my ankle, but when I fell, I landed bang on my shoulder. I'm hoping I've just popped it out, but I've got a feeling I might have broken my collarbone."

"Oh, no, that's terrible! If you've broken your collarbone, you won't be able to work."

"That's why I'm being positive and hoping it's just popped out. But I can't get up, Violet. Every time I try to move, the pain is excruciating. The first time I tried to get up, I actually passed out for a minute."

Concern lodged in her throat, and she reached out and put one hand gently against his cheek.

"Well, it's okay now. I'm here to help. How can I help you up without hurting you?"

"I'll have to grin and bear it. I can't stay out here all night."

'Okay, let's get you up in stages, and then when you're sitting up for a while, we'll try to get you on our feet to walk back to the house."

He gritted his teeth and nodded.

"Do you think I'd be better off going back and calling for help?"

"No, I can get through this. Besides, I want to get Molly home. I don't want her having pups out here in the bush. You never know what's out here tonight."

"Okay, let's go."

***

Joe

Joe had never heard anything as welcome as Violet's voice when he'd heard her call out. He gripped her hand.

"Thanks for coming looking for me. After

180

my rant this morning, I thought you might not even come back."

"We'll talk about that later, Joe."

"Okay, now I've got to stop being a wuss and get up."

"Okay." Violet's hand was warm on his other shoulder and he groaned as he ignored that ever-present surge of attraction that ran through his blood.

God, he had it bad. He was half-crippled with pain, and all he wanted to do was kiss her.

In the bright torchlight as she crouched beside him, he could see Violet in her faded jeans, her white T-shirt hugging her curves. Her hair was pulled back in a ponytail, and her lips were set in a straight line.

"What are we going to do with you, Joe Rossiter? This is the third accident you've had since I've been at your place."

The others were just little scratches." Violet had insisted on dressing a couple of the cuts when he'd injured himself when he was working on the fence.

"Maybe it's because you distract me so much," he said.

"Distraction? You can't blame me for this. I

was nowhere near you when you fell down a hole, you silly man."

"Yeah, but I only came out walking so I wouldn't be tempted to—"

He bit off his words. He'd said too much.

"Tempted to what?" Her eyes held his.

"Tempted to take you in my arms? Tempted to kiss you?"

Even in the dim light, he could still see Violet's cheeks go bright red. She dropped her gaze and looked away from him.

"Not the best time to start being romantic, I guess." he said.

"No," she said quietly. "Not the best time."

"I'm sorry. I shouldn't have said anything. Must be the pain sending my brain crazy."

Before he could move, Violet leaned over him. "Maybe if I give you something else to think about, the pain might ease a little bit." His eyes widened as her head blocked out the torchlight, and for a long moment, her soft lips settled on his.

"Well," Joe said, when Violet lifted her head from his, "I passed out from the pain before. I might pass out from lack of blood to my brain this time."

Her hand moved down from his shoulder and gripped his hand firmly. "I just needed you to know how I've been feeling too."

"Really?" Hope dulled the pain so it was almost bearable.

"Really. Even with a shitty day dealing with all sorts of things, I worried about you."

"We've wasted a few days, haven't we, Violet?"

"I've never felt like this before," she said, "but I do know I can trust you. We've done lots of talking this week. But we need to do more. You need to understand me."

"I'll do whatever it takes, if you kiss me again."

"No, we have to get you home, and look at that shoulder, and we have to get Molly somewhere secure.

"Okay, let's do this."

Chapter 19
Violet

Once Joe was on his feet, it was much easier, although Violet wouldn't want to go through the process of getting him to his feet again. She'd seen how much pain Joe had been in as he rolled over, finally got to a sitting position, and then a few minutes later, she helped him to his feet. His left hand had gripped hers firmly and he hadn't let go. Her skin tingled all the way up her arm, sending a warm feeling down through her chest to her lower regions.

How could one spark turn into this intense feeling of longing for one man a week after meeting him?

It was crazy.

The grip on her hand wasn't just for support; every so often, Joe's thumb would rub against her palm. She turned to look up at him, but his eyes were hidden in the darkness. Every so often, he'd stop, just like behind, and waited for

Molly to catch up to them. His voice was gentle as he urged, "Come on, baby, you can do it."

It seemed like an hour before they got back to the house, and as soon as the back door was open, Joe was inside with Molly at his heels.

"I'm just going to grab a handful of paracetamol, and then we'll get you sorted, Molly."

"No, I can do that. How about you get in the shower. Your clothes are wet, and we don't want you to get a chill. I can sort Molly out while you get cleaned up."

"Thank you. I'll be quick." Some colour had come back into Joe's face now that they were home and Molly was safe. "I thought I'd put her out at the end of your porch, the little alcove down from the spare bathroom."

"That's a good idea," Violet said. Since they'd been back in the light she'd avoided looking directly at Joe. "We can easily close it off with that old door at the other end of the room, the one lying on its side."

"We need to. Last time she had a litter; all she wanted to do was get them underneath the house, so this way we'll secure to start with."

"Right, I can handle that. Go and have a

shower. You won't pass out, will you?"

"I'll go in a minute. Come here."

His voice held a promise, and Violet's nerves went to jelly as she walked over slowly, lifting her gaze to meet his. Joe still had his right arm tucked against his chest, but he reached up his left hand and held her cheek in his palm.

His voice lowered to a murmur as he leaned close. "May I kiss you, Violet, before I go for a shower?"

She nodded wordlessly as his green eyes held hers. Joe's lips took hers gently, and he cradled her with his good arm.

It was as though she had come home and found a place where she belonged. Violet lifted both arms around Joe's neck to hold him close, and it was Molly's whimper that finally broke them apart..

When Violet heard the shower running, she went to one of the linen cupboards out the back, The first day she'd explored the house, she'd spotted a bag of rags in the bottom of the second cupboard, and now she dug deep and pulled out half a dozen old towels.

Wherever she went, Molly was at her heels.

"I know, Molly, it hurts, doesn't it? Come on, we'll get you settled."

She laid the towels in a deep pile in the corner of the alcove, and Molly looked up at her with her big brown eyes, seeming to know that Violet was looking after her. It only took a couple of pats before Molly flopped down and closed her eyes. Violet walked up to the other end of the room, got the half-door that was there, carried it down, and closed it across the opening.

"I'll come back and check on you in a moment," she said, heading into the second bathroom. She scrubbed her hands and looked in the mirror, not surprised to see a streak of dirt on her very flushed cheeks.

By the time she'd scrubbed her face, washed her hands and tided her hair, she could hear Joe out on the porch talking to Molly.

"Who's a clever girl?" he said softly.

Joe as sitting on aplastic chair he'd brought in from the porch and placed chair beside the pile of towels that Molly was curled up in.

Violet gasped. "Already!"

Two gorgeous little pups, all golden blonde the same as their mum were already nuzzled against Molly. Molly's eyes were closed, and Violet could almost feel her contentment.

"A while to go here, I think," she said.

Joe nodded. "Yes, at least another four."

Two hours later after the sixth and final pup had made its way into the world, Joe yawned. His arm was around Violet's shoulder, and she turned him with a smile. She'd kept them going with several cups of coffee, and Joe's favourite toastie as the pups had been born.

"You look absolutely exhausted. Why don't you go to bed?"

His eyes were warm. "I'm going to take some more painkillers and try and sleep this off."

"I wish you'd let me take you into the hospital," she said.

"Maybe in the morning. If they can pop it back in, I'll be as good as gold. With a bit of luck, I'll get Dr Jess. I think she should have a gentle touch."

"Okay, I'll stay out here just for a while and make sure Molly's okay."

She turned quickly and, still needing to be close to him, pressed a firm kiss beside his mouth. "Sleep well, we'll talk in the morning."

Chapter 20
Joe

Joe found some stronger painkillers in the bathroom cupboard, so he took three, drank two glasses of water, and crashed into bed, avoiding hitting his bad shoulder. He drifted straight off to sleep with a smile on his face, but woke suddenly to a loud pounding on the front door, not sure how long he'd been asleep.

"Who the hell could that be?" He dragged himself out of bed and reached the hall at the same time as Violet. She was in her PJs, and her face was dead white as fear fill her eyes.

"What the hell are you doing, you stupid bitch?" An aggressive voice was followed by more pounding. "I know you're in there. I saw you through the window."

As Joe reached the end of the hall, he held Violet back. "Get behind me." He didn't know of it was the painkillers or adrenaline that surged from the need to protect Violet that had taken his pain away.

"Unlock the friggin door, you stupid woman. How dare you bloody leave me. Thought you were a clever bitch, didn't you?"

Joe stepped forward and turned to Violet. "Go to the kitchen. Make sure the back door is locked. I'll deal with this," he said. "I'm assuming this is your ex-boss."

She looked up at him, her eyes wide, and her face pale. She nodded and confirmed his suspicion was correct.

Joe took a deep breath, trying to clear his fuzzy head. "Look, mate. I don't know how you found your way here, but I'm warning you. You've got about ten seconds to get back into your car and get off my property again, or I'll be calling the police."

"Who the hell are you?" the bloke said.

"I'm the owner of this property, and you're trespassing. I suggest you leave straight away. I also suggest that you leave Bindarra Creek and don't show your face here again because if I ever see you in there, I'll knock your block off, mate. You leave Violet alone. I've heard enough about you to know that she can press charges.

"Bullshit, you can."

"Don't worry, she has evidence."

The guy's belligerence faded. "And who the hell are you? She's shacked up with you already. Always knew she had no morals."

"Ten seconds," Joe said. "Get off my property."

All was quiet and then the sound of a car roaring down the drive reached them.

"What a charmer," Joe said as he held his arms open to Violet. She fell against his chest and buried her head on his shoulder. She was trembling uncontrollably, and dragging in short sharp breaths.

"It's okay, he's gone, and I won't let him hurt you."

"How did he find me?" she said.

"Your sister, maybe."

"No, she didn't know where I was when he went there.

"It's strange, unless someone in town made a connection and let him know."

"I know who it must have been." Violet looked up at him, her dark brown eyes huge in her pale face. "Jake must have said something to Emma's dad. He and Brian were great pub mates. And Brian was in Sydney when I left. He must have called around everywhere." Her voice broke. "I knew he wouldn't give up. He couldn't handle rejection."

"It's okay now." Joe kept his voice low and soothing.

"Jake would never believe us because Brian can be such a charmer."

"I told Emma why I left and she said she'd always known what he was like."

"He's gone now." Joe held her close until her trembling eased.

Violet shook her head from side to side. "No, you don't know him. He won't give up. He won't leave me alone."

"Oh yes, he will." Joe's voice was fierce.

I'm going to have to go, Joe. I'm going to leave tonight."

"And you think you'd be safer getting in a car? Remember, you don't have one."

"I know. I'm not thinking straight."

"If you got in any vehicle, do you think he might be out there waiting?"

"He probably is," she said.

"When you head down that road in the morning, it'll be with me in the car with you, and we'll be going straight to the police station."

Violet started to cry. "I have to go, Joe. I can't stay here. I can't stay. I don't trust him."

"And what happens if he finds you in the next place, and you've got no one to protect you? Violet, I love you. I am not letting you go."

Her eyes were full of tears as she turned to him, and Joe held his breath. When she reached for him, and clung to him, he breathed out and held her close.

He couldn't believe the sort of mongrel she'd run from and what she must have been through. The night she'd told him about her ex-boss, she'd brushed it off as a silly mistake.

"I'll look after you."

"What if he comes back here tonight?" she whispered.

"He won't. If he comes back here tonight, all the doors will be locked, and you'll be sleeping next to me in my bed with the bedroom door locked. We'll go and check Molly and then we'll go to bed. Is that okay with you?"

She nodded wordlessly. The only regret that Joe had was that the first night that Violet spent in his bed would be one borne of fear. He desperately hoped that there would be many more happy nights ahead of them.

***

Violet woke the next morning with a warm am draped over her. She blinked and then remember the evens of the night before and she took a deep breath.

Joe had said he would protect her, and she trusted him

He'd said he loved her and she hadn't replied; she had been traumatised. She rolled over slowly, careful not to move his arm. It was the last thing she'd been thinking of as he'd tucked her into his bed last night.

"I'll sleep on top of the sheet, and I'll keep to this side,' he'd offered.

When she shook her head and held her arms up, Joe had groaned and lain beside her.

Violet let her eyes roam over his face. Joe was still asleep and she looked her fill. His long dark lashes rested on cheeks flushed pink from sleep. The pain must have eased because the lines around his mouth had softened.

A wave of love for this man flowed through her and she thought about what he'd said the other morning.

Now Violet believed in love at first sight too. Her own hero on his white horse had found her a place to belong.

Epilogue
Carols by Candlelight -one week later
Violet

Joe had offered to pick up Jake and Emma, and baby Nat, on the following Saturday for the annual Carols by Candlelight at the showground. He already had a baby seat in the shed for when Georgia travelled in his car.

Violet shook her head. "I can't believe you've got a baby seat."

"Well, she's my only niece, and I've looked after her a couple of times. We've gone to the park, and we've had ice cream. It's a bit far to walk from my farm."

Violet took extra care in getting ready for the night. The past week with Joe had been like all her dreams come true. She'd driven him into the hospital the next morning after a tender interlude in his bed, one that still brought a smile to her face. Dr Jess had popped his shoulder back in.

They'd called into the police station, and

reported the visitor of the night before, and were assured of instant action if they ever had any more visits.

It was liberating to have shed her worries; having Joe by her side had eased all of the worry. He'd given up the night job at the pub because he didn't want her home alone.

Her ute repair had been sorted; when Emma suggested she take it further, Violet had been to see the solicitor in town, and sent an email to the car dealership, reminding them of their obligations under the law, and she received an immediate response. Her refund was being processed before Christmas.

She was looking forward to the carols tonight. She loved the whole Christmas atmosphere and how Bindarra Creek embraced it. She had met so many people already, and had spoken to Billie on the phone to let her know what had happened with her ute. Billie said she would be there too with her parents, and she would look out for her.

As they got out of the car at the Showground, a loud crack of thunder rumbled in the distance, and Violet turned to Emma. "Oh, I hope it doesn't rain tonight."

"There's no fear of that," Emma said. "I had a look at the radar. It's just going to rumble around for a while, and then it's going to head down to the coast. We won't be getting any rain out of it. It is hot enough for a storm though, I didn't think it got this hot up here."

"It's more like a Brisbane night," Violet said.

Emma nodded as she got Nat out of the baby seat while the men took the picnic baskets and rugs out of the back.

Violet was surprised to see many cars parked around the Showground and the number of people who were setting up their positions scattered along the grass. It looked as though the whole town was here.

Once they'd bought their battery-powered candles and songbooks at the front gate, they found a space not far from the front.

The school band launched into a spirited rendition of Jingle Bells as Violet spotted Billie a few rows in front of them and waved. Billie had a wide smile on her face. They'd just settled onto the rug when Joe called out. "Nic, Jess, over here!" His arm was around Violet's shoulder and Emma smiled as Violet reached up and kissed Joe's cheek, as Nick and Dr Jess walked across to them. They made room for the other blanket to be spread beside them.

Violet's eyes pricked with tears as the primary school choir began to sing her Gran's happy carol. *'Santa Claus is Coming to Town'*.

"Look at that, sweetheart," Joe whispered in her ear. Violet turned to see what he was looking at. A spectacular sunset of orange and gold blazed though the threatening cloud and a last shaft of light, lit up the primary school band in a halo of light.

Joe's lips were warm against her cheek. "The first of many Christmases together," he whispered. 'I love you, Violet Valentine."

"And I love you, Joe Rossiter. I promise you'll always be my hero."

THE END

Thank you for reading *A Place to Belong*. Reviews are always welcome on Amazon and Goodreads.

About the Multi-Author Bindarra Creek Romance Series

Welcome to Bindarra Creek, a struggling country town where people work hard and love deeply. Set in the picturesque tablelands of New England, Australia, Bindarra Creek is a fictional, rural community full of romance, intrigue, adventure, drama and suspense.

This latest series, **Bindarra Creek Small Town Christmas**, is the sixth multi-best-selling author "series" set in the fictional small town of Bindarra Creek.

Bindarra Creek Small Town Christmas – released 1st December 2023

The Glitter or The Gold – Suzanne Gilchrist (aka S E Gilchrist)
Christmas at the Cyprus Café – Susanne Bellamy
A Place to Belong – Annie Seaton
A Magical Summer - Rhonda Forrest
Destined to Stay – Kerrie Paterson
Home for Christmas – Lauren K McKellar
The Christmas Surprise – Linda Charles
The Gift of Bindarra Creek – Lindsay Douglas

The other romances are as follows:

A Bindarra Creek Christmas Romance 2022

The Mistletoe Wish – Suzanne Gilchrist (aka S E Gilchrist)
The Christmas Jinx – Susanne Bellamy
The Grinch of Bindarra Creek – Lindsay Douglas
Christmas at Forrest Glen - Rhonda Forrest
Mistletoe Magic – Erin Moira O'Hara
Mistletoe and Blue Jeans – Linda Charles
A Clever Christmas – Annie Seaton
Tangled by Tinsel – Phillipa Nefri Clark
A Cowboy for Christmas – Lauren K McKellar

A Bindarra Creek Mystery Romance

A PLACE TO BELONG

A Dangerous Secret – Suzanne Gilchrist (aka S E
Gilchrist)
Beyond the Gate – Rhonda Forrest
Protecting their Destiny – Erin Moira O'Hara
Only She Knew – Linda Charles
Secrets of River Cottage – Annie Seaton
Forgotten Secrets – Susanne Bellamy
A Perfect Danger – Phillipa Nefri Clark

Bindarra Creek A Town Reborn

Take Me Home – Suzanne Gilchrist (aka S E
Gilchrist)
In the Heat of the Night – Susanne Bellamy
No Looking Back - Linda Charles
Worth the Wait – Annie Seaton
With Every Breath – Lauren K. McKellar
Stealing Her Heart – Simone Angela
A Twist of Fate – Erin Moira O'Hara
Promise Me Forever – Juanita Kees

Bindarra Creek Short & Sweet

What's in a Kiss – Linda Charles
My Forever Valentine – Sandie James (not
available)
Pearls and Green Beer – Susanne Bellamy
Full Circle – Annie Seaton
Date with Destiny – Erin Moira O'Hara

A Letter from the Queen – Lee Christine
Love's Sweet Challenge – Suzanne Gilchrist (aka S E Gilchrist)
The Widow Maker – Lauren K. McKellar
Out of the Blue – Noelle Clark

Bindarra Creek Romance

Bindarra Creek Makeover - S. E. Gilchrist
Shadows of the Heart - Lee Christine
Second Chance Love - Susanne Bellamy
The CEO Mechanic - Sandie James (not available)
Reach for the Stars - Kerrie Paterson
Home to Bindarra Creek - Juanita Kees
Stolen Sanctuary - Stacey Nash
Tempting Fate - Erin Moira O'Hara
One More Day - Linda Charles
The Vine - Lauren K. McKellar
The Ghost of His Past - Simone Angela
Joanie's Dilemma - Marianne Theresa
Buckley's Chance - Noelle Clark

Full details on buy links for all books in Bindarra Creek world can be found at:

www.bindarracreekromance.com

Read on for the first chapter of **Larapinta**, Annie's 2023 Ruby Award winning Porter Sisters series novel.

Chapter 1

The McLaren Mango Farm - May

'Ellie, while you're inside, can you grab me one of your hoodies, please? That wind's cool.'

'Have I got one big enough?' Ellie chuckled as she leaned forward and looked out the kitchen window overlooking the veranda. Her sister-in-law, Dee, sat in one of the papasan chairs near the barbeque table looking decidedly uncomfortable.

'Ha ha. Very funny. Wait until you're seven months along,' Dee replied.

Ellie smiled and touched her stomach. 'I've got a few months before I get there. And I'm not having twins. Stay there. I'll grab you a pashmina. It'll be more comfortable.'

The family had gathered for an early evening barbeque, and to the family's joy, Ellie and Kane had announced that James was going to have a little brother or sister in November. They hadn't shared their news until she'd safely reached the three-month mark.

Emma came into the kitchen as Ellie turned to go to the bedroom. 'How are you, Els? I was so excited to hear your news.'

'I'm good. I'm over the morning sickness now. Just. I didn't have it with James, and I tell you what, it's enough to make me think twice about another kid after this one.'

'Mum's beside herself out there. I haven't seen her smile so much since Dee and Ryan's wedding.'

'Kane and I told her a couple of weeks ago. But I've been a bit worried about her. She's seemed a bit down the past few weeks.'

'Dad's anniversary?' Emma followed Ellie into the bedroom.

'I don't know.' Ellie opened the bottom drawer of the chest and pulled out a pretty mauve pashmina. 'Could be. But she came good when I told her about the bub.'

'Are you still going to fly?'

Ellie shook her head. 'No. I don't want to risk it. It took me a while to fall pregnant. We've been trying since before Dee and Ryan's wedding.'

Emma looked down but Ellie caught the glint of tears in her eyes.

'Em? You okay?'

'Jeremy and I are thinking about fertility treatment. We've been trying for a baby since your James was born.'

'Oh, Em.' Ellie held her arms open and her big sister stepped in for a hug. 'That sucks.'

'It does.' Emma stepped back and dabbed at her eyes with a tissue she pulled from her pocket. 'You'd think both being doctors we'd know how to fix it, but—' She lifted her slim shoulders in a shrug.

'It'll happen. Maybe when you least expect it.'

'I'm getting on, Ellie. I'll be thirty-three this year.'

'What are you girls doing hiding in here?' Dru, the youngest of the Porter sisters stood in the doorway. 'Is everything okay?' Her high forehead creased in a frown.

'Yeah, we're good.'

Dru shook her head. 'I didn't come down in the last shower. What's going on?'

Ellie glanced at Emma and caught a tiny shake of her head. 'We're just talking about Mum. She'd been a bit low again.'

'Well, I just copped a mouthful from her. I went down to the dam to tell her that the meat's almost cooked, and she was up a mango tree with James.'

'Oh no. I told her last week not to do that. She'll end up falling out and breaking something.' Ellie folded the pashmina neatly into a square. 'What did she say to you?'

'She told me she wasn't ready to go into bloody

aged care yet, and she'd bloody well climb trees if she wanted to.'

'What! Mum said bloody?' Emma's eyes were wide. 'I don't think I've ever heard her swear!'

'And in front of James?' Ellie frowned as she led the way back to the kitchen.

'No, she climbed down, and kept her voice quiet enough so he couldn't hear from up the tree,' Dru said.

'Well, I guess that's better than how she was after Dad died, and we couldn't get her out of bed or motivated about anything. Good to see a bit of life in the old girl,' Ellie said.

'For goodness' sake, don't let her hear you call her that. Mum's suddenly got this thing about age. Last time I talked to her, she asked me all sorts of questions. I was worried she was sick and not saying, but she assured me she was fine.' Emma lowered her voice as they reached the kitchen, but it was empty. 'Actually, I've been a bit slack. I haven't called her for a couple of weeks. I've been a bit . . . a bit busy.'

Dru frowned. 'Me either. I've been flat chat at work, and we've been eating out most nights visiting all our favourite restaurants before the tourists hit town. What about you, Ellie?'

A surge of guilt ran through Ellie. 'Me either. We called in to her apartment to tell her our baby news a couple of weeks ago, but that's the last time we talked. Now that James goes to pre-school, she doesn't need to mind him while we both work, and Kane goes into town to pick him up in the afternoons if I'm not home. Do you think she's feeling a bit neglected? Maybe that's what prompted the aged care comment.'

'Maybe. I'll take this out to Dee.' Emma took the pashmina from Ellie. 'And Mum's way too young to be talking about osteoporosis, so don't you dare say anything like that to her.'

'I don't even know what that is, Dr Langford,' Ellie teased.

Emma pulled a face at her. 'Maybe she's been spending time at Dee and Ryan's property. I know she offered to help Dee in the house.'

'Hope so. God, Mum's closer to fifty than sixty, isn't she? I lose track. I don't know where that aged care comment came from,' Ellie said crossing to the oven. 'Dru, can you grab the salads out of the fridge and I'll carry the potato bake out.'

By the time the girls had the salads on the table, and Ryan had helped Dee up from the papasan chair and settled her at the end of the twelve-seater outdoor table, Kane and Connor had filled a tray with cooked steak, sausages and onions.

'That smells great,' Jeremy said as he walked up the stairs to the veranda with Sandra and James beside him.

Soon they were all sitting around the table. The three sisters beside their husbands, Ellie with Kane, Emma with Jeremy, and Dru with Connor. Their half-brother, Ryan was beside his wife, Dee. James, Ellie and Kane's four-year-old son sat beside his nan, Sandra.

'Well, how nice is this?' Sandra said with a wide smile. 'It seems like months since we were all together.'

'I know,' Ellie said as she passed the bowl of green salad to Kane to serve out a portion for James. 'Dru and Emma and I were just talking about that in the kitchen, and how we need to get together more often.'

'That would be nice,' Sandra said. 'Thanks, Ryan, just a small piece of steak. No potatoes for me either.'

'I hope you're not on a diet, Mum,' Emma said.

'No, but I've been going to the gym, and doing lots of walking. Just eating sensibly. At my age, you can't afford to put on weight.'

Jeremy chuckled. 'At your age, Sandra? You're still a spring chicken.'

'Thank you, Jeremy. I'm feeling good. Keeping myself busy.'

Emma and Ellie exchanged a glance.

'How long have you been going to the gym,

Mum? Which one do you go to?' Dru asked.

'The one right in the city. I've made some new friends in the classes.'

'That's great,' Ellie said. 'We were worried that we were all too busy, but it sounds like you have been too.'

'I know you all are. I'm proud of how independent I'm getting.'

'And you're looking really well, Sandra,' Dee chipped in. 'I might drive into Darwin and come to the gym with you after this pair are born.' She put her hand on her stomach.

'I hope you don't go too early, Dee. I'll be away for the first two weeks in June. I'd like to be close when the babies arrive, so I can help you out, if you need me, although I'm sure Catherine will be up here too.'

'Yes, Mum's coming up about that time, but I won't knock back any offers of help, Sandra. I'd love you to come and stay. There's plenty of room at Wilderness Station, and you and Mum get on so well.'

Ellie frowned and put her fork down. 'Away, Mum? First, we've heard of that.'

'Exactly, Ellie. I'm your mum. I don't have to report in with all my activities, do I?'

Ellie froze and stared at Sandra, holding back the quick retort that came to her lips. She had always been the fiery one of the three sisters, and this wasn't the time or place to cause a fight. 'Of course you don't.' Ellie focused on keeping her voice even as she picked up her fork and paid attention to her meal as she spoke. 'So where are you off to?'

'I'm going for a walk.'

'A walk?' The three girls spoke almost in unison.

'Where to, Sandra?' Kane asked.

'I'm walking the Larapinta Trail.' Sandra sat up straight and her smile was wide. 'The end-to-end walk.'

***

Sandra Porter sat back and looked at her three daughters. The looks on their faces varied from shock on Ellie's to understanding on her sensitive Emma's. Dru, as usual, was an enigma, but she knew her youngest daughter felt a lot more than she ever showed to the world.

Sandra had known the family would be surprised and that wasn't a bad thing. The girls had supported her through the hard times after Peter's death, and it hadn't been until the truth had come out, and her conviction that he had been murdered had been proven true, that Sandra had started on the long, slow road to healing. She knew the girls still worried about her, and had been prepared for this reaction.

Sandra was at a crossroads in her life. Her share portfolio had taken off and she had some serious decisions to make about her investments. Peter's death and the subsequent investigation had left her in a very comfortable position, but she hated spending it on herself. Frank Nichols, her financial adviser in the city, rolled his eyes every time she gave money to the girls.

'You would get much better returns if you follow my investment strategy,' he said every time she had a Zoom meeting with him. You need to put some of your money into lithium stocks.'

'The best return is seeing my girls comfortable. I like seeing them spend it.'

It was time to make some changes and make a life for herself, perhaps being the matriarch of the family. She smiled. Matriarch? That made her sound ninety.

Ryan caught her smile and he grinned back at her. He was a good man, and she was proud to have him as a stepson, and a member of their family.

Over the past few months, Sandra had accepted that a gap was growing between them, but she knew it was nothing to be worried about. The girls' phone calls were few and far between these days, and she tried not to call them too often. The last thing she wanted was to seem needy. She knew they didn't mean to neglect her, and there was no conflict in the family. In the increasing time she'd spent alone lately, Sandra had spent many nights thinking back to the early years of her marriage to Peter. When the girls were little and they were building up the mango farm, there'd been very little contact with her parents and Peter's family.

That was life. And the family life cycle continued as families grew into their own entities.

Her girls—and Ryan—were creating their own lives, families and careers. When the girls were growing up, they had seen their grandparents in Darwin at Christmas and on family occasions, and that had been about three times a year at best. Each of her sons-in-law had no family—except for Jeremy. His family was in Sydney, but they were estranged. She had been friends with Kane's mother several years ago, but Susan had passed away. Connor had no family either, and Ryan's parents had both passed. Sandra tried to be a mother to the boys as well.

She grinned. Boys? They were all strapping men in their thirties, but each of them cared for her girls, and Ryan, her stepson, loved Dee. She was blessed that they all lived fairly close.

Emma, her eldest and Jeremy both worked at the main hospital in Darwin. Dru and Connor had their own security business in the city and a beautiful apartment overlooking the park on Darwin Harbour. Ellie and Kane, and her adorable grandson, James, lived on the family farm that Kane had inherited from his mother, Susan. It had gone full circle; when Kane and Ellie had married the Porter mango farm came back to the family. Ryan and Dee lived a considerable distance away on their cattle station, but still close enough to visit.

Accepting as she was of her girls' personal lives, that didn't stop Sandra worrying about them. Ellie was busy with James and her helicopter flying contract, and now she had a new baby on the way to think about.

Sandra had been worried about Emma lately; she knew she wasn't happy, but like Dru, Emma was a private person and anything that was bothering her, she would keep to herself, but hopefully share with Jeremy.

Dru was just Dru, and the strongest of her girls. Dru had been in her mid-teens when Peter had been murdered, and she'd gone off the rails for a while. Sandra carried guilt over that; Dru had needed her, but Sandra had been so lost in her own grief she had let her youngest daughter roam free.

She glanced over at Dru and Connor and smiled. Dru had married a strong man who loved her very much.

'Mum! Don't just sit there grinning like a Cheshire cat, tell us what this walk is!' Ellie's question opened the dam, and a torrent of questions followed.

'Who are you going with?' Dru asked. 'And what's this "end-to end" mean?'

'That's a long trek, Sandra,' Connor said. He turned to Dru. 'I walked the Larapinta Trail with Greg when we left the Federal Police. It was cathartic. Sandra, it's incredible, but are you sure you're fit enough? It's over two hundred ks, isn't it?'

'Two hundred and twenty-three, and twelve days of trekking. And end-to end, means just that. You can do partial treks or you can do the lot. I'm doing the full walk.'

'My God, Mum. You can't walk that far! I couldn't walk that far and you're—' Ellie's eyes were wide and she folded her arms.

'And I'm a lot older that you,' Sandra added sweetly.

Ellie grunted. 'You know what I mean. And don't you have to carry everything? A tent and all your food? I read about that trek in one of the tourist magazines at the airport. I couldn't think of anything worse.'

Sandra ignored Ellie as Connor asked another question. 'Which way are you going? East-west, or west to east?'

'The company I'm about to book with recommend the east to west walk.'

'Phew, you haven't booked it yet. We can talk some sense into you,' Ellie interrupted.

Sandra tried to keep the sharpness from her voice, but failed. 'Ellie McLaren. I am not a geriatric yet. I've still got four years before my sixtieth and I am going to do this walk. And if I want to, I'll climb trees with James too.'

The silence around the table was tense until Emma's soft voice chimed in. 'Ellie, I think it's a great idea. As long as you're with a reputable company, and you're supported, Mum, I think it sounds great.'

'Tell us some more about it, Mum,' Dru said. 'It sounds good. I might even come with you.'

'Oh no, you won't. Everyone wants to.' She shook her head. 'Even Frank, my financial adviser in Sydney suggested coming with me. And don't go thinking I'm going to fall in a heap. I've been off any medication for over two years now, and I'm good. Sure, I get sad about your dad, but I've come to terms with it. Where do you think you girls got your strength from?'

'Sorry, Mum. I know I worry too much. So, tell us all about it.'

'I've got two choices. The one like you said,

Ellie, where I have to carry a bit of stuff. But not a tent or all my water. There is another one I'd like to do that's a little bit softer.' Sandra glanced at Connor and chuckled. 'More like glamping, but I don't think I can justify the price of that one. I mean I can afford it, it's just a lot of money to pay out for comfort.'

Dru looked across at Ellie, and they both nodded. Ellie nudged Emma and she nodded too.

'That solves a problem for us. You pay for your trip and we'll all pitch in for the upgrade for your birthday.'

'Really? Well, I won't say no, because I know if you're helping me out, you approve of me going.'

'Good, that's settled then,' Ellie said briskly. 'Happy fifty-fifth birthday, Mum.'

'Fifty-sixth,' Sandra said.

Larapinta is the fifth book in the Porter Sisters series.

Individual books are available from Annie's store or ask your library to purchase.

A PLACE TO BELONG

ANNIE SEATON

Other Books by the Author

Daughters of the Darling
From Across the Sea
Over the River (2024)

Porter Sisters Series
Kakadu Sunset
Daintree
Diamond Sky
Hidden Valley
Larapinta
Kakadu Dawn

Pentecost Island Series
Pippa
Eliza
Nell
Tamsin
Evie
Cherry
Odessa
Sienna
Tess
Isla

The Augathella Girls Series
Outback Roads
Outback Sky
Outback Escape
Outback Wind
Outback Dawn

A PLACE TO BELONG

Outback Moonlight
Outback Dust
Outback Hope
An Augathella Surprise
An Augathella Baby
An Augathella Spring
An Augathella Christmas

Sunshine Coast Series
Waiting for Ana
The Trouble with Jack
Healing His Heart
Sunshine Coast Boxed Set

The Richards Brothers Series
The Trouble with Paradise
Marry in Haste
Outback Sunrise
Richards Brothers Boxed Set

Bondi Beach Love Series
Beach House
Beach Music
Beach Walk
Beach Dreams
The House on the Hill

Second Chance Bay Series
Her Outback Playboy
Her Outback Protector
Her Outback Haven
Her Outback Paradise
The McDougalls of Second Chance Bay Boxed Set

ANNIE SEATON

Love Across Time Series
Come Back to Me
Follow Me
Finding Home
The Threads that Bind
Love Across Time 1-4 Boxed Set

Bindarra Creek
Worth the Wait
Full Circle
Secrets of River Cottage
A Clever Christmas
A Place to Belong

Others
Whitsunday Dawn
Undara
Osprey Reef
East of Alice
Four Seasons Short and Sweet
Follow the Sun
Ten Days in Paradise
Deadly Secrets
Adventures in Time
Silver Valley Witch
The Emerald Necklace
A Clever Christmas
Christmas with the Boss
Her Christmas Star

About the Author

Annie lives in Australia, on the beautiful north coast of New South Wales. She sits in her writing chair and looks out over the tranquil Pacific Ocean.

She writes contemporary romance and loves telling stories that always have a happily ever after. She lives with her very own hero of many years and they share their home with Toby, the naughtiest dog in the universe, and Barney, the ragdoll puss, who hides when the four grandchildren come to visit.

Stay up to date with her latest releases at her website: http://www.annieseaton.net

Acknowledgements

As always, a special thank you to my dear friend and fabulous editor, Susanne Bellamy, and my eagle-eyed proof-reader, Roby Aiken.

A special thank you to Suzanne Gilchrist for coming up with the concept of the Bindarra Creek series.

A Place to Belong
Copyright © 2023, Annie Seaton

www.ingramcontent.com/pod-product-compliance
Lightning Source LLC
Chambersburg PA
CBHW031231210726
48287CB00003B/745